Be sure and check out my other stories in the
Tarnished Lands series.

## The Forgotten Woods Saga
The Harrowed Half-Breed – Book 1
The Progeny Assassin – Book 2
The Mad Wizard – Book 3

# The Harrowed Half-Breed

### A Tarnished Lands Story

## P.A. WIKOFF

This book is a work of fiction. Character names, places and events are products of the author imagination. Any resemblance to characters (living or dead), incidences or settings is entirely coincidental.

Visit the author's blog pawikoff.wordpress.com

Patreon.com/pawikoff

Follow @pawikoff on twitter and Instagram

Facebook.com/pawikoff

Copyright © 2018 P.A. Wikoff All rights reserved, including the right to reproduce this book or portions thereof in any form whatsoever.

Cover design by Marcela Bolivar.

Visit Marcelabolivar.com

ISBN: 0-9990058-2-0
ISBN-13: 978-0-9990058-2-8

# Contents

# Tarnished Lands

In the aftermath of the utopian regime that ruled for over a millennium, famine, chaos, murder and deceit reign in lieu of balance. The pendulum now swings in favor of disorder. The fierce strong-arm the weak, cowards lurk in the shadows like rats, and the wicked take everything that's left over. This is no longer a place for good intentions; this is a place of survival.

# Prologue

## ~Kip~

Kip scrunches his shoulders, feeling quite uncomfortable in his new surroundings. Every resident of Scutter's Landing is looking upon him in a peculiar way, like they don't take kindly to outsiders. Kip brushes his stringy blond hair out of his face. Perhaps it's his nervous tic that drew in their eyes. Whatever the cause, eyes are definitely staring, and not in a kind or gentle way.

He grips his pocket from the outside of his pantaloons, making sure his small pouch of coins is still intact. Pickpockets are everywhere, or at least that's what he keeps telling himself.

Traveling from a far distance has proved profitable for Kip. He is currently in the lowest point of the city of squalor—the underbelly of the sloped streets where all the filth and broken dreams seem to roll downhill and, in some cases, fall from the sky.

Selling the common items of his homeland has granted Kip quite a large sum of money. Well, maybe not that exorbitant for some, but it definitely is for him. Kip feels fortunate for his fortune; if only he is able to get out of here alive.

The seedy dregs line the streets with open hands covered in sores. Each one is begging for water, and by the drop. There is a hundred-year drought in this region.

His eyes cross as he watches a single droplet of sweat run down his forehead and launch off the end of his nose. *Why am I the only person sweating?* Kip thinks to himself. Maybe it's his fair skin that still hasn't adapted to the hot climate. Or, could it be that no one else has any liquid left to spare?

He is on edge, flinching at the slightest of sounds. His steps are slow and careful, as if the ground is on fire.

Kip overhears a ruckus erupting to his left. He knows that keeping his eyes fixated on the ground means he won't have to get involved, even though he always gets involved, much to his dismay.

Curiosity forces him to shoot out a peripheral glance. A leathery-skinned lady is refusing to part with some precious water droplets she has stored in a vial. A beggar tugs on her pack. She manages to pry her belongings away from his filthy grasp. This only instigates him further, and he tries to spit on her. Fortunately, nothing comes out. Finding another solution, the grotesque street urchin proceeds to pull down his ripped trousers and squats, in the hope of producing something else to throw at her.

The smell begins to waft towards Kip. The foul stench possesses that undeniable rotting aroma. Kip covers his nose and regrettably looks directly at the horrific source.

The beggar is having difficulties and uses his own hand to pull the excrement from his body. Some type of larva wiggles off his hand.

Never in his life has Kip seen an elderly woman flee so fast, and he wonders why he isn't right there beside her. Unfortunately for Kip, he can't pry he eyes away from the sight, as much as it makes him gag.

The beggar turns his cold eyes in Kip's direction, holding up a steaming-hot projectile.

This forces Kip's legs to carry him further down the gauntlet of tragically lost souls. Hands brush by his sides, reaching for a handout. Kip flinches as he pushes through them, fearing that they are all infested with larva. It's heartbreaking for him, knowing he has the answer to all their problems inside his pocket, although Kip knows he doesn't have enough for everyone and merely flashing that kind of coin would awaken a trampling mob.

A peculiar sound cuts though all the moans and groans. It is...laughter. Kip wonders how anyone can be joyous in such a place.

His eyes follow the sound and meet the smiling face of a feathered-folk half-breed leaning against a pile of rubble. Kip's curiosity outweighs his sorrow—he has to find out what could make this individual shine so brightly in such a thick layer of rottenness.

Kip jerks and pries himself past the grabby hands. Making his approach cautiously, he thinks this might possibly be a trick, or worse. He doesn't want to think about what worse might be.

The half-breed's human side shows in his expression. His smile grows wider upon seeing Kip's kind face.

Kip notices that the half-breed has a thin layer of feather-like bristles intertwined with his human hair. This is his first encounter with a feathered-folk. Everyone knows that full-fledged feathered-folk never leave the forest, and half-breeds are only seen passing through.

"Hello," Kip says, his voice cracking.

The half-breed doesn't flinch; he just sits there without a care in the world. His feathered-folk features show mostly in his face and in the toughness of his bark-textured skin, though not nearly as predominately as his pedigreed relatives. His clothes are loose-fitting and layered, with each layer meant to cover existing holes in the previous layer.

"I'm Kip. I have a strange question to ask of you...if you don't mind me asking it," he says, taking a knee.

The half-breed lets out a chuckle, then proceeds to get distracted by a flying insect.

*He doesn't appear to be mentally sound,* Kip thinks to himself. He feels horrible even dabbling with the notion.

Kip wonders why he is even bothering. This is the type of story that people pass along back to his homeland—"Young Boy Murdered for Asking a Silly Question of a Degenerate."

"Here goes," he murmurs. "What makes your smile so... blissful? Don't be offended, please. I must know."

The half-breed erupts in laughter; his belly tightens with each burst of air that exits his mouth.

"This is useless," Kip says with a sigh. *Maybe it's me. Always the butt of a joke.* Feeling defeated, Kip turns away and once again puts his hand over his pocket, grabbing for his coins.

Feeling a hand on his shirt, Kip jumps like he is trying to reach the sky. He has a dreadful fear of catching something contagious. Looking back, he sees that it is only the half-breed.

His laughter abruptly stops, though the smile never leaves his face.

The twinkle inside the half-breed's eyes captivates him as Kip moves in closer. *What do those eyes see that I cannot?*

Kip touches the rough hand that holds on to him and returns it to the half-breed's side.

Something drops out of his hand. It's a large black jewel, a beautiful one, in fact.

"Here, you dropped this," Kip says, picking up the gem.

He presses it into the half-breed's palm. A connection is made as magical energy flows through them both. Inside his palm, Kip sees images shine through the gem's finely cut edges, like a whole world is inside and is trying to get out.

Kip's eyes grow wider as he witnesses exactly what makes the half-breed smile...

# A War for All Seasons

~Valara~

The feathered-folk had resided in the wild-woods for greater than a thousand years. They lived off nature's gifts while never upsetting the symbiosis. It was a sacred way of life passed down from each generation.

Soon the humans found value in the forest's wood and sought to cut down the very lands that provided for the folk. Human greed was a flaw that flowed deeply within their blood; they couldn't help it any more than they could help breathing or blinking.

While the humans pilfered more than necessary, the trees bled dark sap, showing their displeasure.

As the self-appointed wardens of the forest, the feathered-folk raged war against the humans. Peace was in their nature, though you wouldn't know it as of late. There hadn't always been conflict between the two bloodlines, although as of the last couple years, it was a daily struggle. With each fallen warrior, contention spoiled their kind nature and poisoned their disposition.

For the last ten years, the humans had brought in huge stones for the purpose of constructing a mighty castle inside the shrinking forest. Stumps scarred the landscape around the monstrosity, and the outer walls were almost fully constructed.

The folk's village consisted of intricately designed burrows, carved out around tree roots. The warmth of the earth protected them in the cold winters and kept them cool in the hot summers. They kept the roots moist and fed, giving back in the mutual exchange.

The feathered chieftess, Valara, whispered a prayer into a hidden artifact for safekeeping and tucked it away into her bag. She launched herself atop a fallen tree, standing tall and proud. "Victory fills our spirits with blood. Tonight we shall push them out with every drop of it. Make the humans remember our sharp faces, as we pierce their eyes with our arrows."

Famished, her folk let out a groan, not impressed with her valiant display. Lately, they were losing the campaign to drive out the invading forces. The human's numbers kept increasing. Fighting them was like cutting a worm in half.

"Their god is not the same as ours. They worship a mortal of flesh and bone, and a heart that bleeds. I have been gifted the knowledge of the man-god's weakness," Valara continued, her hands acting as annotations.

"Look around. The forest wants to die. The humans have already paved their victory," a feathered-folk archer piped up.

"I heard a whisper in the elemental winds. I alone am privy to the secret. It is ripe on my lips. I can taste it," she said, licking her lips.

Once a year, the hot winds from the east blew through the forest, cleansing all forgotten dreams, or that is what they believed. The feathered-folk felt this wind was sacred, and it had made its way through the forestscape three days prior.

Now, she had their attention. The war party took to their feet, demanding for the knowledge to be shared, like a pack of whiny pups.

"Prove to me that you're worthy of it, and it shall be yours," Valara said, wearing a sinister smile.

Screams shook the forest as the feathered-folk let loose their emotional spirits.

One folk couldn't control the power encapsulated inside himself. He slashed at a timid brother in arms, while howling like a wolf.

The mob descended upon his treason, each one making a hole where they could. Soon, every inch of his body had a weapon inserted in it, like a pincushion.

"Enough!" Valara yelled, her eyes panning back and forth eagerly. "It has begun."

All at once, they reclaimed their instruments from his body and blood misted through the air. They all took a deep breath, letting it enter their lungs, believing this to be a blessing from death.

"Weakness is in their young. The man-god sees through the eyes of human innocence. Cut out their babe's eyelids so that they cannot be sheltered from our brutality. They will watch our ways as we peel them like an apple, taking them apart bit by bit. Make their man-god afraid of our bloodline, as we bathe in their tears. His sadness will become silence when their prayers come to call. On this glorious night, while the moon is black, the humans will be forsaken by their god!" Valara declared with conviction.

The war party screamed and took to the woods. It was the time of Necrosis, the last of an aging moon.

Valara led the charge as they stormed into the darkness of night, toward the half-built castle.

Upon reaching the clearing, they winced at the starlight as if it were blinding their eyes.

A feathered one wept upon seeing the devastated forest ridge. "I used to climb the trees here. They were the tallest around. Now, it's nothing."

Valara doubled back only to cut him down with her chiseled stone sword for divulging their weakness to the humans. "Keep this place in your dreams," she whispered, making sure no one heard. Her strength alone empowered them to fight.

Forest-made weapons clashed with the steel and bronze weaponry of the avant-garde humans. The young feathered-folk dragged their dead and wounded back to camp. Sometimes it took two or more to manage the task.

Each human captured was made an example of—diced and drained—despite any feelings of abhorrence.

"Metalmen!" a feathered man yelled, with a human child tied to his chest.

The humans had armored knights that were difficult to fell. Under normal circumstances, it could take six or so folk to take down one knight. Tonight proved much more favorable, and it only took three lives for a knight to succumb.

Fire scorched through their ranks from a burning catapult positioned behind the castle. Both sides suffered. Starlight reflected off the blood-puddles that were forming.

Valara was taking victory home with her that night; she swore it so. Every cut satiated her thirst for revenge.

When the humans first came, they held the white flag bearing peace. Many agreements and trades were made between the two factions. That was until a new lord came about. His lies and trickery taught the humans to take instead of asking, punish before reason, and murder above trial.

The feathered ones believed that the humans had been infected by the curse of greed from this new lord, and feared that they wouldn't stop until no trees were left to mourn.

The folk were succeeding in taking back their homeland one death at a time. The cries of the human children invigorated their assaults.

Valara's personal bodyguard, Vox, had claimed the most lives that night. That was until he met Lord Neff and his mastery of the sword. That was the first moment she saw the new lord—as he slayed her best inside the inner sanctum of the unfinished castle.

They knew his name well because he spoke it after every execution.

"Neff!"

There went another one.

Valara knew that if Neff could defeat Vox, he could slay them all. He was the only thing standing in her way. His contagious curse infected the whole lot of humans, and she was determined to cure them *all* with her blade.

With each side's numbers thinning, Valara knew she had to take it upon herself to end this battle once and for all. She never took her eyes off Neff, meeting his weapon and sneer head-on.

They smashed weapons, his epee against her stone longsword. His technique seemed almost unbeatable.

He easily found an opening and slashed her arm. The sting hurt less than the truth that cut deep within her—she couldn't beat him, not alone anyhow. She cried out for assistance, although no one was free to heed her call.

Valara opened herself up to his blade, looking at her folk fighting valiantly.

Always greedy, Neff wasted no time driving his blade through her; ecstasy shone on his face.

This action disarmed him long enough for her to thrust her stone longsword into his chest, matching wound for wound.

"Your god will witness this display and fear us," Valara said.

"On the contrary," Neff countered, as he pulled her weapon out of his chest, seemingly unaffected by the same pain that plagued her.

Neff then removed his own weapon from her chest and wiped it clean with a rag already soaked in blood.

Upon seeing their leader fall, the feathered-folk started to retreat.

Valara screamed, hoping to grant them her fighting spirit, but she wasn't so lucky.

"And now, I have a gift for *your* gods. If we cannot drive you out, we'll shame you out," Neff said. With a wave of his hand, his people barricaded the remaining forest dwellers inside the keep. Outnumbered and trapped, they were beset with death.

A human priest closed her wounds with his healing prowess, just long enough for her to live through more of Neff's torture.

"I'm sorry," the priest mouthed, wincing as he performed his witchcraft.

Valara hoped to die before Neff finished exerting his dominance over her body. She begged the priest for mercy with her tarnished eyes, where mercy meant only an end.

Fearing the lord, himself, the priest granted no such request that night.

Before daybreak, Neff released Valara and her remaining folk back to the woods. He had bestowed a dark shame upon her, along with his message, "Here is my kindness: never set foot on our side of the forest or else you'll witness my less merciful side."

Seven feathered-folk had witnessed the evil that had transpired that night, and Valara made sure only her most trusted three made it back to camp alive—Bae, Merim and Lancer.

Valara was disgraced, demoralized and broken, though her secret was safe...for now.

# After Effect

~Valara~

Months eroded by and famine had developed throughout the tribe. They had kept out of the eastern forest, heeding Lord Neff's warning. This resulted in less food, water and supplies. Normally, during this time of year, they would gather berries and fallen nuts from the east.

Valara had her own emergency provisions stashed away, and she was making quick work of them as of late. One day, while reaching for her stash, Valara had trouble squeezing into the cove. She thought this strange, as she had entered her secret hiding place many times before without any issue. She ran over to the glowstone that illuminated her private cleft. Sure enough, there was a lump growing inside her belly. Even though her wounds from the battle had healed, the pain was far from done taking its toll.

Valara slowly took out her stone longsword and placed it on the table. She lifted a boulder that she often used as a chair and rested it on top of the sword, holding it down.

Valara knew this was his doing, and it had to be undone. Her shame couldn't stay hidden forever, unless it was buried with her death.

She slowly removed her armor, piece by piece. Feathered-folk armor was made from rare shells that could be only found underground. They were large, jagged and strong. Humans customize their metal to fit the shape of their knights, whereas feathered-folk start wearing their shells before they're fully developed, and their bodies mold to their armor's will. It's a rite of passage known as "mard" and, more often than not, the armor outlasts its host.

Removing the armor, she noticed how much tighter it had become. She took a moment, caressing her bulge with her hand.

She felt grief tickle her eyes as she thought about the next life.

Quickly Valara snapped out of it and ran into the blade, letting it stab her stomach. She reached out, grabbed the boulder and pulled the blade deeper inside.

Her eyes filled with liquid as she tried to fight the pain. She had to be absolutely positive that she struck the living tumor.

"I'm s... " she couldn't bring herself to apologize.

Her screams shook the air as she pivoted her hips, tearing the hole sideways.

Hearing her deafening cry, several feathered-folk rushed to her aid.

"What assassin could do such trickery?" one onlooker gasped.

"Don't touch her; leave her be," Lancer said, holding everyone back with her arms. Lancer was one of the trusted three that held on to Valara's secret, and she knew exactly why the sword was lodged inside her abdomen. "We need a witchdoctor. Go, now!" Lancer yelled.

Lancer cleared everyone outside of the underground cleft.

"Oh, Valara... we have to tell them. You cannot lead in this condition," Lancer said.

"I would rather perish."

"You may get your wish," Lancer said, with a shaky hand.

"I've taken care of it. I'll never let them get the upper hand; our survival depends on it."

"They already have it. Can't we open up negotiations again?"

"You heard that monster. Never again shall we set foot on their side. It will only further our casualties. No, we have to regain our strength, regroup, before it's too late," Valara said.

"What happened to you?" Lancer asked, shaking her head side to side.

Valara stood there in silence. She wanted to answer the question as truthfully as possible, but doing so would crush the small amount of pride she had left.

Without warning, the witchdoctor burst in holding healing herbs and bugs alike, treasures from the forest used to extend life, numb pain, and clot blood instantly.

Valara felt cold and numb while the witchdoctor carefully removed the stone sword from her belly.

After the witchdoctor treated her front and back wounds, Valara was then ceremoniously dressed, and buried up to her neck. It was a standard practice for the feathered-folk, although seemingly strange to outsiders if they were ever to witness this unspoken ritual.

Before the week's end, Valara had enough strength to pull herself out of her body-grave. Her bark-like skin had been repaired. She wasn't fully healed, however. The bastard child still grew inside her, determined to live despite her efforts.

Valara would not leave her cleft as the months wasted away. She was depressed and hiding her affliction as it grew.

Hoger, a stout warrior and Lancer's mate, barged in without an invitation or greeting. "I've come to relinquish you of your leadership."

"Traitor," Valara said sharply, eying her weapon merely an arm's reach away.

"Everything is falling apart. The trees are bleeding more than ever. Something has to be done, and it cannot happen from the underwoods."

"I'm waiting for the wind to answer my call for recourse."

"You're past your time. Hand over the gem," Hoger demanded, with eager hands.

Valara stared him down with the intensity she thought she had lost on the battlefield.

Hoger felt a shiver upon his spine, and he wondered if she was stronger than he had expected.

"Come take it, if you dare," Valara said, snatching her stone sword.

"I will destroy both of you, if I have to," Hoger said.

"If you can," Valara spat. He knew her secret; Lancer wasn't as trustworthy as she had thought. "Lancer will be my next victim for breaking a vow."

"Lancer knows? Here I thought I was the only one," Hoger said, touching the club that was stowed on his back.

"How did you find out?"

"I saw you at the lake yesterday."

Her lower spine ached and only the weightlessness of swimming gave her relief. Due to the poisonous waters, Valara thought it to be a perfect spot for privacy.

"You leering creep," Valara said, standing up, unveiling the true extent of her growth. The parasite that kicked and clawed her from the inside protruded outward like a fist, amplifying her strength.

Pointing her stone sword at Hoger's head, she knew it was a swift blow away from silencing him forever. She pulled back, preparing to do just that.

Hoger released his hand from the hilt of his weapon. "I want no trouble. Something just has to change around here to calm the unrest."

She knew he was a coward, and sometimes you need a coward to grovel at the scraps you feed them, keeping them fed just enough to remember what hunger is.

"You can't hide that thing any longer," he said, staring at it without daring to blink.

"If I take your eyes, there will be nothing left to witness at the lake or otherwise."

Hoger slowly shuffled his feet backward. "You're powerless outside the prison you've built for yourself here."

"Do you really think you can make it out of here alive?" Valara held in a deep breath, steadying her body.

The cowardice that he normally tried to keep hidden leaked out of his pores.

"Hold on. Let's help each other. You need to keep your secret...secret, and I need a leader to address the current issues," Hoger stammered.

Valara stood there unaffected by his plea, keeping her aim on her target. Inside her mind, she gave him ten seconds before ending him.

*1...*

"If Lancer became chieftess, she could handle all your affairs while you came to term with your...transformation," he wept.

*...4...*

Valara knew that Lancer was much more of a threat than the sniveling male who stood before her.

*...8...*

"I'll do anything!"

*...10.*

"Okay, Hoger, I elect you as my standing second. But know this, I'm watching you, and if you mess up, I'll leave a huge mess for Lancer to clean up."

"What? Me?"

"I need to depart to the Flower Grove. You're in charge until I return."

"I wasn't expecting such an honorable appointment...thank you! I won't let you down."

"Coming here today, you've already let me down once..."

"What do you want me to do?"

"Leave."

"Then what?"

"Lead."

Hoger left with visions of his own greatness dancing in his mind. It didn't take long before reality set in. His leadership was worse than mediocre. He kept on wondering why things wouldn't just go his way. It was the push-pull of leadership. Not everyone could be happy at once; some had to starve to prevent others from suffering. Having to make those choices made Hoger feel like a god, though he never got the respect of one.

# Unexpected Bundle

~Valara~

A frost crept through the forest. It was the coldest day of the century. Valara held an icy leaf between her fingers. It crumbled like something different; it was softer, more delicate. The elements had changed it somehow. She wondered if she was also affected by the coldness of the Flower Grove.

In the spring, every trunk in the grove was covered with a tiny flower that only grew out of the tree bark. It was a magical place which had long since fallen dormant with biting winter. Now, snow capped the trees, making them seem no different than the rest of the forest.

The beauty and happiness this ancient place brought was replaced by despondence and dread. Even the warmth flowing through her body didn't faze the everlasting chill.

She knew today was the end of the festering blister that lived inside her—that's how she thought of the thing. Once it popped, she could begin to heal from the inside out.

Her hand shattered the leaf as a sharp, stabbing pain squeezed her from within. It was coming, and like the dawn of a new day, there was nothing she could do to stop it.

After thirty-six hours of kicking, screaming and scratching its way out, she finally gave life to a baby boy. The forest was the only witness to her shame.

Without even looking at it or wiping it dry, she left it out in the elements for a numbing goodbye and went back inside her shelter.

The infant's cry awakened something inside her—a nurturing nature. She longed for the beast, to cradle it and comfort it. She refrained, holding herself down with a strap, no longer trusting what she was capable of doing, or in this case, not doing.

Valara thought that if she waited until it stopped wailing like a banshee, she would be free from its curse.

It kept screaming for what felt like an eternity...until it stopped.

Valara rushed outside, breaking the strap. She just had to make sure it was all over—her shame, her disgrace, her uncertainty.

The blood and fluid coating the demon was already frozen over. Even the afterbirth was hard as stone.

A powerful punch of regret hit her so hard that she forgot how to breathe. She scooped up the babe into her arms, applying it to her breast. It wasn't taking the bait.

"Shhh, come on, you wretched thing," she said, gently tapping its cheeks.

It was too late; she had abandoned her offspring far too long. He felt like a block of ice pressed against her bare skin.

"I'm s...orry. So sorry."

Something froze under her eye. She quickly wiped it away before the gods of the forest could see. It floated down like a tiny snowflake and landed upon the infant's nose. At that very moment, the babe latched on to her, full of life and spirit. The forest was watchful that day, and she thanked them...secretly.

The winter continued to stalk them like an assassin—slow and cold.

Valara called the babe "Barnacle" because he was always attached to her, though she never actually felt burdened by him. She hid his non-folk features under a winter cap.

He was a leech, sucking the life out of her, or so that's how she convinced herself she felt. The truth was something she couldn't ever admit—it was almost like the child was filtering out the evil set deep inside her. She even smiled on occasion, though she was always quick to cover it with her hand. In actuality, he was her finest gift from the world, given out of the worst of all her days.

Spring was approaching. One of her three trusted servants barged into her cleft.

"I'm starving," Merim declared.

"Everyone is," Valara said in a hushed tone, not wanting to wake the sleeping bundle in the crook of her arm.

"He isn't!"

"What do you want me to do, feed the whole tribe?" Valara spat, looking down at her chest.

Merim paced back and forth, trying to keep his blood moving, to keep warm and irate.

"Three folk died just this week, and that little monster is getting portly like a pig."

"He takes from me, not the tribe."

"You think I don't notice how much you eat now, but I do...and I'm not the only one."

"Are you blaming me for those deaths?"

"I should just tell them all of your little 'disgrace' and be done with it."

Valara gave him a horrifying gaze while reaching into her fur-lined sack. "Half."

"Half what?" Merim questioned with a skeptical eye.

Valara tossed over what was left of her daily food ration.

"Fine. Just keep that thing clear of me," Merim stomped out of the cleft.

Each meal, Valara took half of her rations and stored it inside a woven basket. At the end of the day, she placed it outside her cleft for Merim. This was the price she had to pay to safeguard her secret and for motherhood.

When spring arrived, the shortage of food didn't melt away with the snow like past years. Times were changing, and the humans were to blame.

As for Valara, her body wasted away. Her muscle turned to empty skin, and her bones felt brittle, though the baby still grew healthily. She had been sucked dry. The suckling took from her, even when she had nothing left to give. Her skin cracked like a drought-laden lakebed.

His hungry cry pierced her ears and infected her soul. All she had left was her own food. Still not weened, he was frustrated by how arduous the adult method of eating was, never getting full as fast as he was used to.

Finally, he closed his little eyes, moisture still on his red cheeks. Valara placed him inside a sleeping nook she had carved out of the wall for him. She covered the hole with fur, hiding it from the rest of the room.

Valara needed to find a better, more permanent solution in order to provide for her young. Starvation wasn't an option. She knew that if she were to perish, Barnacle wouldn't be allowed to gain his own portion—he too would succumb to hunger.

Valara snatched the remaining morsels of her food allocation and took to the surface woods. On her way, she was met by Merim.

"Where do you think you're going?" Merim asked.

"I need to feel the sun."

"You look bad."

"Of course I do. I'm malnourished."

"I didn't say I felt bad."

"What do you want?"

Merim looked overly healthy and quite plump around his center. Valara noticed that he was no longer wearing his shell-armor, for obvious reasons.

"Your portions are getting smaller."

"No, you're just getting bigger."

Merim stuck out his chest, trying to make himself look fierce. Little did he know that it only made him appear obese. "What do you got there?" Merim asked, pointing at the sack of scraps tucked inside Valara's hand.

In that moment, Valara seriously considered killing her compatriot, which *would* give her access to the rest of her allotment of food. Her only hesitation was that she held no weapon. Valara pondered the consequence of failure—*who would care for the little angel?*

"It's the babe's waste. You want it?" Valara said, shoving the sack at Merim.

"No, get that thing out of here," Merim snarled, grabbing his nose.

Valara slunk away from the engagement, only pausing once to reconsider the option of murder.

Deep inside the dark forest, Valara laid out the finest cloth she had over a scarred stump. Carefully, she placed her remaining nourishment in a pleasing arrangement. She then hid inside the trees. Her bait was set; her trap was ready.

She waited...and waited. Nothing came. The bait was tempting her to take it for herself. Her own hunger was plotting against her better judgment. If it weren't for her uncharacteristic drooling, she may have never noticed her own insanity on the matter.

Hours went by uneventfully. She bit down on her arm to keep her mouth busy, until a large rodent came lurking, smelling the sweet aroma of her berry bread. Its nose twitched, guiding the vermin closer to the stump of goodies. Valara's hand shook as it gripped a jagged rock in the ready position.

Once in range, she threw the rock, smashing the rodent's head, knocking it to the ground.

Valara scampered to the kill on all fours, like an animal. She quickly concealed the creature inside her pack.

She knew that she had committed a high crime of the forest. Meat and insects were only allowed to be consumed if they happened to die of natural causes, and there was no way she could justify the bloody gash on the creature's head.

Regret and worry consumed her as the full extent of her actions weighed on her conscience. She had just put her folk and spiritual beliefs below the needs of her child—a half-human child.

Suddenly, she heard the sound of shifting feet off in the distance. They weren't made by someone who wanted to go unnoticed.

Valara hid in the tree's shadow, anticipating her own downfall. The forest spirit had seen her blasphemy, and payment was imminent, she thought. Gazing at her weak arms, she knew that she didn't have the strength to best anyone.

Keeping herself hidden in the tall grass, she quickly started to feed on the rodent, each bite inciting the next. Warm blood ran down her chin as she tore through the meat with her incisors. Her fingers clenched the inedible bowels and intestines, keeping them separate.

Time had run out. Her challenger had arrived, but it wasn't a feathered-folk...it was a human.

The man peered at the picnic curiously, before kneeling down at the foot of the spread.

Both of them were far from each other's homeland, and with no dividing line, either one could be considered trespassing.

Valara knew she was in deep. She couldn't let him steal the last of her baby's food, not after she ate all the meat she had caught for it. Still shrouded by nature, she called out, "That's mine."

The man stood up, holding the berry bread between two pinched fingers. "Who's there?"

"Please go away."

"Show yourself, or else..." The man placed the bread up to his open mouth.

"You wouldn't dare." Valara's muscles tightened as anger manifested from inside her.

He answered by showing her exactly how daring he was. The flavorful bliss brought forth emotions upon his face as he rolled his eyes back, further adding insult to injury.

"Mmmm, so good," he said almost inaudibly, his mouth busy with the bread.

Valara launched at the man, throwing the bloody pelt as an appetizer for her punishment. It hit him squarely in the face.

Lost in the quickness of the events, the man was knocked to the ground, still struggling with the wet remains touching him.

Valara's frail body loomed above him as she dug her claws into his throat. Her teeth felt as if they would shatter from her tight-jawed expression. She thought deeply about her child's lamentation and mustered enough power to pull the cake out of his neck, killing him instantly. She used both her hands to re-form the cake into its original square shape. It was no use; it was ruined with saliva and human gore.

She threw it down and closed her eyes, mentally preparing herself for what had to follow. This crime was far worse than killing a creature of the forest. This was breaking a truce which was forged on the threat of extinction.

Blood stained the air. She had to think fast, before the carnivores were attracted to it.

After digging a pit inside the soft soil, she found some nearby vines and wove them into a rope, wrapping them around the man's feet. Blood drained out of his body and into the pit below. Valara chipped and filed a stone until she had crafted a razor-sharp point.

It took the rest of the daylight hours, but she managed to separate the man's meat from his bones. She disposed of everything inside the pit, except the meat, leaving an unmarked grave behind.

Dirt had stuck to the rodent and man blood that drenched her whole body.

Her back ached as pains shot through her. It wasn't up to the physical task she had put it through. She staggered all the way back to her dwelling with the large sack strapped to her. Luckily no one was paying attention as she sneaked back into camp. It was far too quiet, even for nightfall.

Upon reaching her cleft, she couldn't stand anymore and collapsed to the ground, releasing the cargo from her back. Without thinking, she closed her eyes.

"No. I can't." Valara crawled to the table and used it to pull herself to her feet. She looked around and realized that her belongings had been rearranged. Someone had been there in her absence.

She limped over to the nook where she had left her babe, holding her lower back for support.

*As if this day could get any worse...*, she thought, as she violently forced her body to the wall. She ripped open the fur covering and found her majestic prince still sleeping...like a baby.

She smiled deeply and, for that moment, all her pain evaporated.

Her happiness was fugacious, as her work wasn't nearly done. She rubbed salt throughout the pile of thinly sliced meat in order to keep it from spoiling. The friction of the salt grains wore through her fingertips. Salt burned her open wounds, though she pursued on until her task was concluded.

She hid the forbidden meat in the only place no one would dare look for it...under her child's dirty waste coverings.

There was one final task that needed to be addressed before her quiescence—the bloody evidence that covered her completely.

With a stone dirk, she gently peeled the top layer of her bark-like skin clean off and gingerly placed it in a pile. Each peel was agonizing torture. Even gazing upon her boy couldn't numb the suffering, although it helped her resolve.

Once she had cleansed herself, she escorted her skin shavings to the high-peak where she gave her offering to the wind.

"There is nothing I won't do for him," she whispered as part of herself blew away.

# Secrecy

~Valara~

Valara feasted on the cured human meat while giving the child her own food allocation. It was the exigencies of their survival. This lasted until her child grew into a juvenile.

During this time, she had become a recluse. She justified her lifestyle, *simple and alone, inside our own.* Her only contact was with her offspring, as no other beings could ever live up to the standards he set in her eyes. The truth, however, wasn't purely speculative.

Sadness surrounded the camp which was on the brink of starvation. Still, veiled laughter was often heard creeping out of the underground crevices, haunting the deprived.

Disconcerting voices spoke in hushed tones, never voicing their contention publicly, until one day when Hoger requested an audience with Valara...and kin.

She feared how she would seem to them, as she felt different somehow. She entered the once immaculate throne room, which was now disheveled and in disrepair.

Hoger lounged on her oaken throne with little concern for his untidy appearance. Lancer stood tall next to him, with a puzzling look upon her face. An amalgamation of lesser folk and guards worked busily in his presence.

"Greetings," Valara said. Forcing the words out brought a sting to her ears. She was still not settled with having been manipulated into giving up her tribe to Hoger. She knew that she just needed to gain enough strength to take it back.

"Where's the child?" Hoger asked brashly.

Valara looked around at the company in which he gave no regard to secrecy. Brief silence fell upon the spectators' curious looks, though they were quick to return to their responsibilities.

"I...don't understand?" she said awkwardly, forgetting how to act with her own kind.

"Lancer, be a dear and fetch me that child."

She gave him a reluctant nod.

"Wait. I'm still the chieftess of this tribe. I relinquish Hoger of his duty," Valara said, every word feeling forced as they left her lips.

"You dare to challenge me? You're weak and frail. I gladly accept," he said bounding to his feet, blindly reaching out for someone to toss him his trusty rock hammer.

Valara reached up high, holding the black gemstone that granted her the rite of chieftess.

The room fell silent in the presence of its ample power.

Hoger twitched his irritated fingers at the sight of the artifact. He wondered why his weapon hadn't been reunited with his eager hand.

The maul was held by a confused guard who internally deliberated his next course of action. Making a false move would undoubtedly cost him his life, if he wagered the victor incorrectly.

A more loyal guard sliced off the hand that held his master's weaponry, releasing it to the floor.

Even with the loss of a limb, the guard didn't make a peep, fearing losing more of himself if he did.

The full mass of the heavy maul was heard by all as it crashed on the floor, shaking the whole room.

It took both hands and all his bodily strength to reunite the hilt with his master's hand.

Hoger wielded it one-handedly, pretending he could do so with ease. What courage Hoger lacked, he gained by the massive weapon.

He approached Valara heavy-footed.

She scanned the room, wondering how much loyalty still sat with her, if any. Lancer was once a trusted friend and companion. There was a time where her support against any foe was unconditional; though now she was unsure. Valara knew that folk followed fear and strength. She also knew that she had, unequivocally, lost both during her absence.

Lancer continued making her exit, not wanting to pick a side in this engagement.

Valara knew that she couldn't beat him, not for sure, anyway. She had to protect the thing that meant the most to her in the entire forest.

She pointed the black gem directly at him. The torchlight reflected off its sharp edges and onto his face. Mystified, he stopped his advancement.

"I concede," Valara said, dropping to her knees, offering up the artifact. Keeping her eyes on the floor, she winced as she felt the gem roughly ripped from her hands.

It was over for her; she had nothing left to bargain with. She looked up with her pouting eyes to see his sinister, self-adoring grin.

Through her peripheral vision, she noticed Lancer's shadow lingering in the hallway.

"Please," she whispered.

"What was that?" Hoger gloated.

"Please!"

"Answer me one thing. Who's the father?"

Valara squirmed with a trembling mouth, caught off guard. He didn't already know. She was grateful to learn that Lancer still had honor—if not for Valara, for her word.

"You don't even know yourself, do you?"

Her shameful shrug was enough to appease his curiosity.

"Lancer, I've got something more pressing for you to address," he commanded.

Valara's old friend made her way to the now legitimate chieftain.

"Take this filth out of my presence!"

Lancer's frown told her tale of woe, as she heavy-handedly dragged Valara away like a commoner.

"And know this, if she ever crosses my sight again, I expect her to be slain before I have a chance to blink," Hoger concluded, as they left the chamber.

It wasn't her life Valara was concerned about; it was the life she had made. If she lost, she didn't want to think about his fate. All that mattered was that he was safe. But how long would that last?

Upon reaching the entrance of her cleft, Valara felt strength return to her weak knees. "Unhand me."

Lancer released her grappling hands, giving Valara back her independence. "What have you done?" Lancer scolded.

"What I had to."

"No, you should've died long before bringing that demon into this world."

"I tried. You were there."

"You should have tried again, and again, until you succeeded," Lancer said slowly, over-exaggerating each word.

"You don't know what I've been through."

Lancer shoved Valara into her cleft.

Valara staggered, almost losing her footing and dignity.

"See, even now you're not willing to fight back. You gave up long ago."

Valara held her head down, knowing that she was right. There was a time the tribe was all she was, all she had. Nothing could have penetrated her preservation of their bloodline, almost like an addiction.

"That human really did a number on you," Lancer scoffed.

Valara felt her fight return momentarily upon hearing Lancer speak ill of the child.

"He's only half human! Don't forget that he is also one of us!" Valara launched at Lancer's throat and overwhelmed her to the floor.

Valara's grasp tightened, leaving Lancer's mouth gaping and struggling to breathe.

As fast as she had gained her strength, she lost it when she caught the eyes of innocence peering out from behind a curtain.

"Oh, dear," she said, rushing to him.

"Valara!" Lancer snarled from behind, her voice wounded.

Slow and refined, the protective mother turned around, once again with great power behind her movements.

"I wasn't talking about the child. I was talking about the *noble* lord. He is the one who weakened you, and you continue to weaken us today."

"Get out of my sight," Valara said with a stare that could kill a man.

"Our alliance is finished. My debt to you dies today and, if it comes to it, I will end your misery myself. So, let the spirits witness my testimony." With that final word, Lancer was gone.

Valara knew she had to leave, and there wasn't any time to pack trivial things. She had to just grab the boy and flee to the outer ridges of the forest. She turned to her offspring, forgetting the anger that still filled her eyes.

The boy stated crying loudly. For the first time, he saw his mother for what she used to be—a force of evil and suffering.

Quickly her face turned soft again, though it was too late; his fear wasn't so easily forgotten.

She tried to console him, but the closer she got, the louder he cried.

"Shhh, darling," she pleaded.

The screams echoed off the roots and rock, alerting the whole tribe to his presence.

His sorrow was crippling. She grabbed her ears to mask the torment.

Her cleft filled with feathered-folk, each one shocked to witness the lies and deceit of their once powerful chieftess.

She wasn't so naive as to think that things could go on like this forever, but it ended faster than she had hoped.

All she could do was sit on her knees and rock back and forth, hoping for something to end his sadness. Something she couldn't provide for him.

Finally, a guard scooped up her child and extinguished his cries with his palm.

Valara reached for Barnacle. She hurt from the pit of her stomach, from where he used to be a part of her.

Guards bound her hands behind her back.

Her sockets couldn't accommodate the influx of liquid any longer, her vulnerability no longer concealed.

She watched herself become nothing as they were separated...forever.

# The Pack

~Barne~

The bastard child was brought to the custodian, Nanis, whose duties included, but were not limited to, rearing the young. His cocked head exposed his concern as he gazed upon this mysteriously old child. Something was different about this one, he knew. Wondering if his old eyes were fooling him, Nanis grabbed the frightened child by the arm, taking a closer look.

Running his hands through the soft growth on the child's crown confirmed his suspicions. There were no buds sprouting where they ought to be. He wasn't a folk at all; he was an imposter.

"Excuse me," Nanis cried out to the guard.

"What's the problem?" the guard asked, annoyed that Nanis had interrupted him while admiring his blade.

"Where did this child come from?"

"The old chieftess. Why? Is it damaged or scarred?"

The little one's eyes looked up at Nanis; innocence defeated duty.

"Uh..."

"Well, spit it out. I'm already late for patrol, and my blade is getting hungry."

"Doesn't he have any belongings?" Nanis came up with the first acceptable truth he could generate.

"Of course not. The traitor hid this child slave inside her cleft, for...years maybe."

"Okay."

"That's it?" the guard asked, narrowing his inquisitive eyes.

"Yes. Thank you."

"Old bark. Wasting my time with his wasteful words," the guard said, watching his own lips move through his blade's reflection as he walked away.

The magic of young often penetrates the inner pits of the good. Only the truly wicked can resist their charms; and Nanis was no more evil than anyone else in the tribe.

"What have we got here?" he asked, using distorted glass to inspect the child closer than his tired eyes could.

It didn't take long for Nanis to realized that this was no imposter, it was a half-breed—half human, half folk. Never had he seen a half-breed reach this length of existence. In the past, any and all half-breeds were either executed on sight, or left outside of the confines of the forest. They never grew to such an age.

Half-breeds were born with the fundamental features of the folk, along with the blood of their other halves flowing freely through their veins, softening their bodies. This resulted in wondrous opportunities for their kind—not limiting them to the same restrictions the full-bloods had to contend with, though it also served as a detriment, blocking them from the inherently enchanting effects of being a pedigree.

"Can you walk?" Nanis asked, noticing that the child seemed to be standing on its own.

Not being an expert in half-breed affairs, the elder had no idea how old it was or how developed the kid should be.

Never having left the confines of his mother's spacious cleft, he felt alone and frightful. Reluctantly, he took a couple paces, and did a full turn on his heels, never taking his eyes off Nanis.

"Excellent. You understand me, don't you?"

The child's expression was unfazed by the question.

Nanis was intrigued by the rarity of his new-found subject. "What's your name?" he asked, wondering if the child was brought up outside of their customary methods.

The child thought about what his mother called him, and until this day, he had never had to say his label out loud. "Bar...nacle," he struggled to make it sound the same way his mother did.

Nanis hedged, wiping his chin, confused. His assumption proved correct, as young folk are normally without an identity. "No, that's not a name—it's a parasite. We will call you Barne from now on."

The boy wondered what a parasite was, and why he wasn't good enough to be called one. Surely his mother thought more of him than this stranger.

"All right, off to bed, Barne."

It took a moment before he caught on to his new nickname and followed Nanis into the next room.

Nanis spent the next couple months keeping the half-breed isolated from the rest of the children. He had to teach him more about their society and language. Barne was much larger than his full-blooded counterparts. Nanis knew he had to work hard to get the half-breed's aptitude higher than his peers, in order to blend in.

He even applied a drying agent to Barne's skin to make it more bark-like, along with giving him a cloth coif to hide the human features upon his head. In the dimly-lit underground, he was passable, but in the unforgiving daylight of the surface side, he knew there would be no disguise short of magic that could hide the truth.

Not wanting to be seen as playing favorites, Nanis knew he had to change something before his new ward began attracting attention.

"Barne, do you see yourself as different than the other kids?" Nanis asked.

"Sometimes."

"Why is it that you feel this way?" Nanis poured himself some warmed river water.

"Because they all live together, and I live here with you."

"And why do you think that is?"

"Because of my ma?"

"No, never think that. You get no special treatment, you hear me? You are exactly the same as the other kids. No one should suspect a thing," he said, flustered.

"If you say so," Barne said, removing his cloth hat, getting ready for bed.

"Don't ever remove that, even while you sleep."

"But why?" he asked, jerking his hand away, thinking it a peculiar demand.

"Because folk might think of you differently, if you do. You understand me?"

"I thought you said I wasn't different?"

"What did I tell you about thinking for yourself. Don't think, just do exactly as instructed."

"Is it good to be different?"

"No, it's bad, extremely bad. You are the same. Say it."

"I am the same," Barne said, pulling his hat down past his eyes.

"Good. Now you're ready to join the others, don't you agree?"

"Okay." Barne peeked out of the head covering.

"This means we're not friends anymore. Not that I don't care for you, it is quite the opposite, really. You have to treat me like the rest do. Contain your feelings, and you will be just fine."

Barne jumped into Nanis's arms without notice, almost knocking him to the ground.

"What did I just tell you?"

"I just wanted something to remember you by."

Nanis squeezed him tightly, conceding to the sentiment.

They soon arrived in a dark room, where the air was cool and crisp. Holes in the ceiling let the sparkling light from above inside. It was the first time he had even caught a glimpse of the outside world. He breathed it in deeply—it smelled like endless possibilities.

Nanis gave the lad bedding and an empty place on the floor to curl up on.

"Goodnight," Nanis whispered.

"Nite."

"Remember...you're not special."

Everything was dark and damp. He spent the next of couple hours missing his mother more than ever. He thought of her until slumber brought her smile to life within his young mind.

Barne spent his first dew timid and doubtful of what to expect.

The morning light brought life to the other children's eyes. Within a flash, they all scattered like a bunch of insects. Each one bore a different task.

Barne watched with scared amazement out of his leaf-woven blanket.

*Who are all these people my size?* he thought to himself. *And how did they learn to move so fast, with such purpose?*

His leaf blanket was ripped off his body, letting the cold morning air sweep over him like a tidal wave. Before he knew it, some little person had neatly folded it and stowed it away, along with everyone else's.

He brought his knees to his chest, scared of judgment. Deep down, he wanted to help, to blend in, although he figured he would just get in the way.

Feeling the touch of another child's hand upon his shoulder caused an almost electric surge to flow through Barne's body. It felt comforting and soothing. He wondered if this was what acceptance felt like.

"You're new here, huh?" the child asked him.

Barne slowly nodded.

"Just find something to clean."

"Clean?"

"Yeah, like removing dirt or leaves. Or better yet, see all that moisture? It needs to be collected into those buckets, with a cloth," the child instructed, pointing at a pile of dry rags that were used to wipe down surfaces.

"Why?"

"Just move your body swiftly and look like everyone else, because right now, you're going to get us all in trouble for being an idle."

"What's an idle?"

"Hurry, someone's coming," the child said as he moved Barnacle's body around like a puppet until he continued the motion on his own.

Barne wasn't really doing any work, but the child was right, he also wasn't sticking out anymore.

Nanis barged into the room and paused, taking notice of how the newcomer was faring. He was pleasantly surprised to find him cleaning with his new brothers and sisters—or at least that's what he thought he was observing.

Within the eighteen hours of their workday, Barne learned how to care for the vast root system that grew throughout their subterranean village, though he got lost at almost every turn. The other children moved fast, talked fast, and hid fast.

"Psst...you're in sight," a girl child whispered to Barne.

He looked around trying to determine the origin of the sweet little voice.

An adult male barreled through the corridor, shoving him out of the way. Barne let out a squeak, thinking the worst was over.

His noise alerted the adult to the true crime that was happening in front of him.

"You..." the adult yelled with a scratchy undertone, "...shouldn't be seen!" He pulled out his bow and aimed it at Barne with the intent to kill.

Right then, a small hand pulled Barne into the shadows and down a small hole, just as the arrow took flight.

The bow, never intended to be used indoors, or at such close range, caused the projectile to ricochet off the very spot Barne had stood a moment earlier. It came back and nearly nailed the archer multiple times.

"You have to be more careful," the girl whispered.

"What did I do wrong?"

"We are the wind—they hear us and feel our presence, but we're never to be seen. Only Nanis is allowed to have any direct contact."

"That's because he's so blind, he cannot see us anyway," a third child said out of nowhere. "Let's go. It's time for fungus detail."

At the end of the first day, and every day afterward, Barne hurt from head to toe with cuts and bruises from god knows when and god knows what.

The children were an integral part of maintaining the village. High energy, strong work ethic, accompanied by their tiny bodies, made them the perfect candidates for the job. They were fearless, even while working in dangerous places.

It was believed that their diligence was a rite of passage. They were told that preforming such backbreaking work for table scraps would grant them an opulent adulthood. Each one believed it, even though no one around lived a life quite as depicted.

Gossip among the kids was the fastest traveling thing within their world. From lips to ears and back again, whispers of Barne's near execution was echoed from the halls and caverns. It was his punishment that had him commissioned to the waste room. This was considered the worst chore, and it could only be done once the adults had turned in for the night...for good reason.

The smell scrunched his nose, and narrowed his eyes.

"We've all done it before," a girl with bright feather bristles consoled him.

Her words were met with confirming nods from the rest of the dirt-covered faces.

The waste pit was at the lowest section of the village. The ground gave way to each of Barne's unsure steps. He held a flat-headed scooper and penetrated the pile, releasing a gas that choked him momentarily.

"Now into the sack," a child yelled from a safe distance.

Barne pulled the heavy sack off his shoulder, releasing it with a thud. Opening the drawstring, he shoved the waste-covered spade into the sack. Something grabbed hold of the tool, not letting it go.

Using all his might to pry the scooper out of the bag, he fell directly on a pile of moist fecal matter. He wanted to die at that very moment.

"Hurry! Get scooping!" a voice rang through the pit.

Barne awkwardly tried to get another pile, when suddenly something ferociously slithered out of the bag.

The dimly lit area didn't give much insight as to the location of whatever he had released. A slurping and munching sound shook the hall.

Slipping and sliding on body fluids, Barne tried to make his way back to the encouraging cheers from the other children.

His inquisitiveness forced his head to look over his shoulder. What he saw was a hairy slug chowing down on all the excrement the tribe had produced.

Keeping it contained was the only way to guarantee no loss of life from this masticating menace.

It circled around, blocking Barne's retreat. Inspecting his clothes, Barne knew he had to remove his tunic, which was covered in what the slug thought of as food.

With each bite, the rubbery skin of the beast expanded in girth. Already, its circumference was ten times larger than the sack it had come in.

"It's eating too much," a child pointed out.

The beast moved towards Barne like a rippling wave. He was forced to back away further and further from his exit, and threw his tunic into its mouth. The thing gobbled it up like a mere appetizer.

An echoing alarm rang through the hall.

The children froze as the sound got louder. "Someone is awake. Get out of there!" they cried.

Barne looked up and noticed hundreds of shafts on the ceiling. He knew that something foul was about to descend upon him.

Not knowing which of the holes was going to unleash its terror, Barne dodged and weaved around, hoping that if he kept moving, he might be spared the humiliation.

A soup-like consistency descended directly toward him. Paralyzed with fear, he covered his head as it rained down upon him.

The giant slug stretched out and caught the fresh snack inside its mouth, saving Barne from being drenched with filth.

Barne moved out of the way before the belly of the beast came crashing down, flattening him like a leaf.

To the half-breed's amazement, the entire room had been licked clean by the beast. It turned towards him slowly, not yet full. He scrambled left and right, but it slithered after him with purpose.

"Shoes! He wants your shoes," another kid instructed.

Barne kicked his foot coverings right into the sharp jagged teeth of the beast's mouth.

The slug stopped for a moment as something different started to happen.

The room began to quake as it opened its hideous mouth twice as wide as Barne's entire body. Black mucus dripped from its upper teeth onto its lower ones as it gathered an incursion of air, almost pulling the child into its maw.

It let out a huge wave of gas right into Barne's face, causing him to roll backward. Mucus and slobber coated his whole body, and a horrendous smell filled the whole chamber.

"Ewwww," the children said in unison.

The slug closed its many eyes and curled up in a coil, like a snake.

Barne met up with his compatriots. Excitement erupted among them, though they were wary to come close to the boy.

"That was easy," Barne said, trying to make light of the incident that had nearly killed him.

"Wait, how are we going to harvest the thing now? It's raging out of control," the oldest of the kids chimed in, muting all congratulations that were in progress.

"What do you mean?" Barne asked, wiping the sticky substance off his face.

"We need to harvest it," a young boy explained.

"What do you need in order to do that?" Barne asked, searching his mind for a weapon mighty enough to slay the slug.

"We need the slug's waste in order to feed the roots of the forest. If it gets contaminated, it will prove worthless."

"Get my bedding. I have an idea." Barne said.

Before any more questions were asked, a few of the kids disappeared up the pitch-black caves.

By the time Barne had finished wiping all the chunky mucus off his body, the group had returned with his leaf bedding.

Barne started to make his way back inside the hall.

Some kid grabbed him by the arm, forgetting where it had been. "Don't go back in there. It's dangerous."

"I have a plan."

Barne approached the beast on the very tips of his toes, trying not to make any noise. It was the largest creature he had ever seen and took up half the room with its quivering body. He couldn't figure out where the worm-like thing started and where it ended.

He knew this wasn't going to be easy, as he placed his hand on its taut skin.

Gasps from the children broke the silence.

Fine hairs stuck between his fingers as he tugged hard, finding little to no give. Not wanting to chance waking the sleeping giant, he amassed as much hair into his palm as he could and used it to pull himself on top of the thing.

The monster shifted slightly, causing Barne to shuffle, losing his balance. He steadied himself, waiting for the beast to calm down. From this vantage point, he could see a flap, which he deduced as the creature's waste slot.

He made his way to the area on all fours, trying hard not to make the thing stir again.

The tip of the tail was much smaller than the rest of its engorged body, though he still wasn't strong enough to lift the thing.

He draped his blanket around the flap and waved his hand, trying to get the attention of his peers. He had an ingenious idea but knew he couldn't execute it alone.

No one was responding to his plea.

Again he waved, this time with both hands.

Each kid shook their head, not wanting to jeopardize their own life for this newcomer who was attempting to get himself killed for the third time today.

On his own, Barne had to do the very thing he had hoped to avoid—he had to wake the beast.

The youngster carefully wrapped both his hands around a single hair. Closing his eyes, he saw the face of his mother who always gave him strength. He tightened his grip and pulled with all his might, ripping the hair out of its pore. Pink liquid squirted out, and the beast started to unravel itself, in hysterics.

Barne then crawled under the slug, attempting to reach the thing's tail before it started to rampage. He did his best to hold himself and the leaf bedding in place.

The slug dragged him through the chamber with little concern for its own proximity to the walls. It was only a matter of time before the beast crushed him accidentally.

All of a sudden soothing notes slowed the beast's movements. The music got louder as the chorus grew. The monster was distracted by the harmonious song, and it started to return to its coil.

Barne used this opportunity to finish wrapping up his make-shift diaper. He wasn't fast enough, though, and he saw the world around him being replaced by the fleshy skin of the slug.

Climbing the beast from the inside track was much harder due to the little amounts of hair on its underbelly. Right when he thought he had met his end, a hand extended down from above. He grabbed a hold of it without thinking twice. Sliding out, his foot caught on the center of the spiral. One tug later and he was free.

"Thanks," Barne said breathlessly as soon as they were at a safe distance.

"No problem. You were really brave," the kid said, also catching his breath.

"What's your name?"

"I haven't got one," the boy explained.

"Why not?"

"We don't need them. We should just blend in, unseen."

"I see you."

"Seyu…I like that name. But please don't tell the others, okay?"

"Okay. I'm just thankful that it had hair for me to pull."

"That isn't hair. It's parasites."

Barne thought about how the hair follicle had wiggled around when he had pulled it out. He knew that the boy's words were true. "So that gross thing is a parasite? Is that what she thought of me?" he said under his breath.

"What was that?"

"Nothing."

Barne and Seyu walked over to the rest of the group and the soothing song they made through pursed lips. Barne didn't know how they made such a sound, but it was amazing to him, nevertheless.

Once the beast was completely asleep, their whistling faded into a hum, then to nothing at all.

On the way back to their sleeping quarters, Barne was approached by the largest kid of the group. "How is your bedding going to stop the slug from making waste?"

"Yeah, it isn't nearly strong enough," another kid agreed.

"It isn't going to stop it; it will collect it. Someone used this technique on me when I was really little," Barne admitted.

"I've never heard of such a thing. Is it going to work?" one kid said in amazement.

"We will know tomorrow," Barne said.

"If it doesn't, I'll feed you to it myself," the largest kid threatened.

Barne curled up in a ball and shivered most of the night away, unable to sleep.

He felt something warm cover his body. It was too dark to know who was showing him kindness, but he took it with a hidden smile.

In the morning, Barne watched as his new friend Seyu delicately folded up half of a woven leaf blanket.

Work continued, just like every other day, starting with dew collection. It wasn't until midday that Barne heard a whisper that his plan had been successful. His bedding kept the beast's waste separate from the folks' and was easily harvested while it napped.

The worst of all jobs had just become the easiest. They all swore an oath of secrecy about this new development. They didn't waste their new-found free time; they allocated it for an outlawed activity...play.

Each night another child donated a small fraction of their bedding to Barne, showing their faith in him.

Barne wasn't used to the long hours expected of him—grueling hours, mostly on manual labor—hauling boulders, fortifying the underground shafts, and feeding the massive subterranean roots. The work seemed more physically demanding to him over the other kids', for some reason. He tried to reason with himself that his body would miraculously adapt at some point. However, it never did.

As folk children, they were never allocated a proper food ration. Instead, they ate spoiled food or scraps that fell on the floor. This didn't prove to be enough for his aching belly. All the years of sacrifice his mother made had him accustomed to half of an adult-size portion.

His inner rumbling announced his discomfort to the pack, and he always tried to hide it with a cough or pass it off as flatulence.

While fortifying the east corridor, Barne found loose dirt underneath an old post and opted to investigate the cause. He crawled inside the hole, which was slightly smaller than he was, shifting and digging with his hands.

Once he couldn't move any further, Barne opened his palm, shedding dim light from his glowstone. He shook the rock with frustration. Every other folk would activate their stone merely by standing close to it. Barne thought his was impaired. As a result, it only glowed while he touched it. He winced as his eyes adjusted to the brightness.

Hordes of beetles scattered from its radiance. Their pincher-like feet tickled his face as they crawled all over his upper body. He swatted at them, dropping his light source; it went out instantly. Even though he could no longer see the buggers, he felt them everywhere, using his body as a thoroughfare.

One smashed against his arm above, falling into his mouth. He coughed and gagged, but the bug went right down his throat.

Though horrified, he tasted a familiar flavor—one he actually craved from time to time.

He calmed his body and opted to leave his defective stone, exchanging it for a fistful of beetles.

After managing to back himself out of the hole, he held the insects inside his palm for the rest of the day, despite how much they tickled his skin.

Later that night, Barne brought his treat to their nightly run of "Out of Sight." It was a game where everyone hid and tried to pelt someone else with a rock, before getting hit themselves.

Barne was late that night and everyone had already disappeared into the shadows.

"Guys...psst..."

A rock came after him from the shadows. He managed to dodge out of the way, barely.

"I have something important," he pressed.

Two more rocks came at him, both hitting him dead-on.

"Ouch, come on."

His words were overshadowed by giggles.

Barne retired outside of the play area, waiting for an audience.

Another rock hit him smack-dab in the head, causing him to drop the beetles on the ground.

"I wouldn't do this to you guys!" He scrambled on all fours, more concerned about catching one of his fleeing treats than the illegal throw.

It was too late, they were already gone, and without his glowstone, there was no way he could re-catch them.

Feeling defeated, he hid in a corner until the game came to a close.

"What's wrong, Barne," Seyu asked, while everyone else was making their way to bed.

"I had something special to share with everyone, but no one would listen."

"Is this what you're looking for?" Seyu asked, opening his hand, presenting a squished beetle.

"Yes! Where did you find it?"

"I saw that it was important to you, so I hunted one. But it got squished...by...someone else."

"It doesn't need to be alive," he said, blowing the dirt off its broken exoskeleton.

"What's it for?"

"Eating."

"Excuse me?"

"I think my mother used to feed them to me."

"Mother?"

Barne cracked the shell open, exposing the soft interior. He held it up to Seyu's face.

"No, I can't."

"It's not gross at all." Barne broke it in half and put some inside his mouth with a crunch. "See?"

"It's not that. It's forbidden. No creatures of the forest can be killed for personal consumption. We have to try and not be selfish."

Barne wondered why his friend was okay with squishing the bug but not eating it. "Who will even know?"

"The forest gods will. Nothing hides from their watchful eyes."

Barne was starting to become aware of the rules his mother undoubtedly broke for some reason. He wondered if she was a traitor, or perhaps a heathen. All he could remember was that she was sweet, kind and loved him very much. Until he started to remember their last meeting. She looked like a demon, with eyes of fire. He started to feel embarrassed about his actions, as he lowered his hand.

"Don't tell me you like to eat those things?"

"No, I just thought we could try it, for fun..."

"Don't worry, I won't tell." Seyu brushed the beetle out of his hand and walked away to meet up with the others.

If what Seyu said was true, Barne knew he was already in trouble with the forest. Maybe it was the human blood flowing through his body, but he quickly picked up the beetle and tossed the rest into the back of his throat.

# Exile



Valara, the once brave leader of the entire tribe, was at this moment reduced to a task fit for the wounded. She had been relocated to the outskirts of their land. If you had a folk that wouldn't fall in line, yet didn't warrant public execution, this is where they went.

When in power, she had also used this location to make problems disappear. Now she was the problem. Only, under her rule, she would have punished herself far worse. Hoger talked tough, but in the end, he didn't think about consequences. Valara planned on teaching him that lesson someday soon.

Valara was given a nighttime position sorting through acorns that had been foraged in the light of day. A slow and steady pace was what she was known for...until everyone turned down for the night, at which time she gained a burst of energy and hastily moved her fingers like crawling spider legs. Doubling her production granted her a couple hours of spare time.

Valara didn't squander this time away for leisure. Instead, she chipped away at a secret tunnel—in hope of reuniting with her son.

There weren't any tunnels that connected her new home with the main village, where her Barnacle was. It was for good reason. The midway stones were harder and difficult to deal with. This didn't deter Valara. She had determination, reinforced with certitude. She would only let her body's cessation slow her down.

The months chipped away, as she kept up this ritual. It was becoming extremely difficult to hide her rubble evidence. One morning, while getting ready for sleep, she overheard an acorn gatherer complaining about something.

Valara tried to make out all that she could, though most of it was muffled. "There seems to ****** dirt down here. Fresh dirt."

Muted laughter.

"No, ******* maybe a cave-in. ***** by the east entrance."

"How should I know ****** said."

"**** much harder **** stone fragments."

"Okay ********** tomorrow it is."

She knew they were talking about the excess rock she had been hiding everywhere, as she wasn't allowed to leave the work area. Not knowing how much they were on to her, she knew that she had to find another way to camouflage her venture.

The next night, she spent half of her free time quarrying away at the tunnel, and the remaining time grinding the shards as finely as she could. It was very time consuming and arduous, but a necessary step for her clandestine plot.

Once finished, she had scarred the floor into a bowl shape from all the rock grinding she had done. She brought a handful up to her face, inspecting how fine it was.

Thinking about her darling child, alone, she filled her mouth with the coarse dust, forcing it down her throat. Instantly her mouth felt dry and raw. Some of the rocks were still jagged, and she felt each one inside her. She continued this process until the pile was completely gone.

Her stomach hurt worse than when she had stabbed herself, though it didn't sway her from eating the stuff the next night and the night after that.

She continued to smuggle her mess, using her body as the vessel, passing it in the place where no one would ever ask questions...the waste pit.

As the rock scratched away at her insides, the solitary life scratched away at her mental stability. She often caught herself talking to the air, and hoping for an answer. She needed a friend, and she knew she had none within her own people.

She wondered how she had let everything fall apart, the tribe, her legacy, all her loyal subjects, her beautiful little one, and now her body.

One day, while sorting acorns and talking to the air, she heard a voice speak back to her.

"Hello?" the high-pitched voice said.

"Who is that?" She turned around swiftly, wielding her carving rock for protection.

"I'm right here," the voice said, seeming closer this time.

Valara slashed at where she thought it had come from, but no one was there. She wasn't friendly enough with any of the gatherers to warrant them playing a trick on her.

"Come out so I can see you. This is your last chance."

"You won't hurt me," the voice said with a giggle.

"Don't taunt me. I'm warning you."

Laughter erupted even louder this time.

Valara was ready to murder whatever it was just to make it stop. Searching and searching, she couldn't locate the source of the voice.

"I'm following you!" it taunted.

"What did I say?" Driving her mad, she brought a rock to her ear in the hope of ending its torment the only way she knew how, by deafening its voice.

It was then that she saw it. A small mouth on her other hand was speaking to her. Dropping the sharp chipping-rock to the ground, she extended her arm as far as she could without ripping it from her body.

"How did you get there?" she asked.

"You put me here."

"No, I did not!"

"Either you did, or you're losing your mind. Which would you prefer?" the mouth asked.

She studied its movements and knew she had seen those lips somewhere before, but she couldn't recall where. Knowing that she wasn't at all crazy, she accepted the fact that a mysterious being had somehow manifested upon her body.

"What do you want?" she queried the hand.

"What everyone wants, to bite someone's throat out," the voice said, chattering with delight.

"Not everyone wants that."

"But you did at one point, didn't you?"

"Well, not anymore," Valara said, picking up the jagged rock again.

The hand took control of the stone and brought it to Valara's neck. Valara used her other hand to fight against the mouth that sought her harm.

Bashing the hand against the table caused acorns to fly everywhere; the rock released from its clutch.

"See what you did!" Valara yelled, picking up the rock with her other hand this time. Now that the tables were turned, she was ready to smash it.

"Stop!" the hand pleaded.

"Why should I show you mercy? You didn't show me any."

"Because I'm a part of you now."

"Not anymore!"

With her knee pinning down her wrist, she drove the rock into her hand and proceeded to saw into it. The pain was mirrored by the cries the hand made. She almost felt sorry for it. Almost. The limb would have been completely removed if she hadn't started to run out of energy. Perhaps it was the pain, or the full belly of rocks, but she collapsed to the floor.

"I knew you couldn't do it; not like I would have," the hand chided with a gleeful undertone.

"Maybe tomorrow you won't be so lucky," she snarled.

The next morning, Valara awoke not nearly done with her sorting. Acorns were everywhere, and the sun was about to crest over the horizon. If the gatherers found the mess, she would be done for.

Thinking it was all a bad dream, she glanced at her hand. Seeing the scabbed-over wound forced her to reconsider.

As fast as she could, she collected the acorns and placed them on the table. She was ready to do the impossible when she heard the voice again.

"You haven't the time."

Fearing the obvious, she looked down at her hand...the mouth was back. "This is all your fault."

"You tried to kill me. You may never reach your son if you only have one hand. You really need to think these things through."

"You're not helping," she said, trying to do her task single-handedly.

"Are you going to be nice to me?"

"Do I have a choice?"

"That's nice enough," the voice responded.

Her mouth-hand started to flop around on the table like a fish.

"What are you doing?" she asked, pulling her hand up, trying to gain control.

"Helping," the hand said, chewing a mouth full of acorns.

"Are you serious?"

"You have a better idea?"

She sorted the acorns while the hand ate as many as possible. This continued right up until the next shift awoke. She quickly slipped into bed and closed her eyes, still chewing on a mouthful.

# Obeying the Law



As the years progressed, Barne felt less and less accepted by his peers. He started to look, think and act differently. He felt as if they were constantly judging his ideas and purposefully going against them. As they aged, the children wanted to keep more and more to their traditions, not venturing too far off the beaten path and risking falling astray.

One week out of the year, the children were tested to see if they had mentally and emotionally matured. If selected for advancement, they were given a name, armor and accepted into the fold—and for the first time in their lives, they would finally be "seen."

Witnessing friends ascend to adulthood bred a competitive environment among the eldest kids.

Barne had been passed over for two years now, and the whispers were that his uniqueness was to blame. The truth was far more contemptible; Nanis alone decided who got the ennoblement, and he still wanted to protect the half-breed for as long as he was able.

Barne dreaded becoming one of the full-fledged members of their society. The thought of harming another person frightened him—even the soulless humans.

He was also worried that the higher the status he gained in the tribe, the closer to the forest's eye he would be, and judgment would ensue. As it was, he had violated their rules every single day with his blasphemous bug snacking.

He was living a double life. One where he existed only to survive, like that of a slave. The other, of a gluttonous, greedy thing who took as much as he could and more.

He had a strong appetite for breaking the rules, but always felt horrible after the crime had been committed. This huge feeling of remorse had forced him into a depression. He would curse and snarl at himself for being too weak for giving in to temptation. When this happened, he called himself a parasite and pinched his arm until he couldn't stand the pain any longer. Even then, he would find fault in that he wasn't able to endure more punishment. It was a vicious cycle of self-loathing that got worse with every single day.

He was destructive, and everyone in his pack noticed. Barne saw it too, though he couldn't restrain himself any more than he could stop himself from breathing.

Today was another selection day. Seyu had been chosen as "one of the lucky ones."

None of the "unlucky" children were invited to the ceremony. Seyu was instructed to collect his belongings and meet topside—the place where no child ever sets foot.

Seyu was the only kid that had stuck by Barne throughout his years in the system, and he wasn't going to let a small guideline (which is how he thought of the rules) get in his way.

He shadowed his friend down the corridor, as he was led to the main tunnel leading up. Guards lined the path, making it nearly impossible for Barne to follow. Frustrated, he made his way back to their dormitory. They slept very close to the surface, even though they never ventured out that way. A wooden-grate ceiling looked down on them as they slept. Barne knew that snow and rain often fell through those grates when nature punished them.

If the outside could come in, he could get out the very same way, he figured.

He ran and jumped, grabbing hold of the grate above.

A much younger child walked into the room at that moment. "Hey, what are you doing?"

"Nothing. Just mind your own," he said, swinging back and forth until he achieved enough speed to kick at the grate.

"You can't do that. Why are you doing that?"

"Scat," he said, giving it another try—this time harder.

He finally broke through a beam. The crashing wood slat narrowly missed him as it plummeted to the ground.

The kid's mouth was stuck open like a statue.

As he swung himself on top of the grate, his coif slid off his head. Never had a day gone by that he had been seen without his signature headpiece. Years of ridicule and teasing for wearing it so often had never pushed him far enough to remove the thing. Only now, in a moment of happenstance, had the thing fallen off. Barne had to make a choice—continue with the facade of the past, or move on toward the unknown.

The child's eyes widened before he rushed out of the room, screaming for help.

He felt the freshness of the air as he climbed up the shaft. Almost reaching the top, he felt something attacking his face, something hot. His eyes winced at the brightness of it all.

"Get back down here!" Nanis called from below.

He remembered the kindness of his old mentor and didn't want to get him in trouble, although he thought about how long ago that was and how Nanis barely looked at him anymore.

It was too late, the crime had been done, and he could only move ahead. He knew a punishment was imminent, regardless of whether he returned now or after the ceremony; he had to see this through.

Reaching the surface made Barne feel even more trapped. The light blinded him, the seemingly endless open air was daunting, and the looming trees seemed angry and vengeful.

There was much more life than he had ever imagined. Not just insects, but feather-and fur-covered things darted, hopped, dashed, flew and climbed through the trees without a care for him. It was like a whole world, hidden for years, was just a short climb away.

A soft bed of leaves and needles covered the forest floor. Barne was so used to keeping the likes of both out of his under-dwelling that he felt almost filthy gazing upon them. Every step made a sloshing echo that made him uneasy.

All these emotions and more were spiraling out of control inside his adolescent mind.

To keep moving, he looked for the ceremonious event, though he had no idea where it would be. The outer world was unfathomably large.

Soon he heard a drum thumping off in the distance. He followed it as though it were calling to him. Reaching the site, he was just in time to see his friend finally bestowed with an adult name.

"Let it be seen, by the forest and the gods of the spirits, that this youngling shall forever be called—by friend or foe, through love or hate—Piranis.

"Piranis? He's Seyu," Barne snapped under his breath, settling under a tree.

"Do you accept your place among the tribe?" the extravagantly dressed speaker asked.

Seyu nodded, lacking all emotion.

"Seyu!" Barne cried out, startling some doves that roosted in the tree above. Scared, he covered his ears as the birds flapped and cooed.

Barne's emotions had gotten the better of him this time. He never meant to be so brazen, or even so loud.

A spear flew past Barne's head. The sound of it slicing the air snapped him out of his daze. He knew this was a warning; warriors were trained to hit something even smaller from a farther distance. He looked down at his friend who seemed genuinely glad to see that Barne had witnessed his evolution. Seyu was standing near a guard who had just lost his weapon.

Taking to his feet, Barne stumbled through the forest, looking everywhere for the hole he had escaped through.

Spears and arrows alike flew by him. Barne wanted to stop and explain his situation, but it was no use. His speed was the only thing keeping him from being riddled with wounds.

He knew he couldn't outrun them forever. These were warriors of many seasons, and he...wasn't good at anything, really.

It felt like he was going in the wrong direction as the trees were becoming fewer and farther between. Soon, he arrived at an open clearing. The whole area was covered in round objects roughly the size of his fist. They were scattered as far as his eyes could see. He knew they weren't fallen fruit as the landscape was now void of trees.

Catching his breath, Barne sat on a stump, not knowing what it was or what significance it held. To him, it seemed like a perfectly good seat, and he used it accordingly.

Hearing the snap of a twig, he turned his body. Suddenly, he was face to face with a painted warrior holding two throwing spears.

"Come with me, you snoop," the warrior instructed.

Barne looked around, confused. He didn't think escaping would warrant sending an armed guard. It couldn't have been worse than eating the sacred insects, although he never actually got caught for that.

"This is a dangerous place. You shouldn't be here," the warrior continued.

"Right now, nothing seems more dangerous than those two spears," Barne said, crawling to the other side of the stump.

"I'm putting them down," the warrior said, crouching.

A cracking sound rang through the air, as an unknown force tore through the sky. Like a fast-moving cloud, its movements were elegant and precise. A bluish tail streaked behind it. It was like nothing Barne had ever seen.

The warrior's eyes looked as if they were going to jump off his face. His hands were in a frenzy as he encouraged the boy to flee with him.

The force increased in speed, striking the warrior in the back.

Barne winced, and when he reopened his eyes, there was nothing left but colored mist evaporating into the air.

Barne gripped on to the stump tightly, aghast of what he had just witnessed. He didn't move or blink until a busy bird's song returned life to the forest.

Still fearing the sky, Barne crouched down and made his way over to the two spears that were left for him. One of those round objects lay between them, exactly where the warrior's feet used to stand.

He wondered if that magical force was turning folk into spheres. Looking around, he realized what it meant if his hypothesis was correct. They were everywhere! The real weight of the loss was overwhelming.

He reached down to collect the sphere, which was still moist, when....

The birds suddenly fell silent.

Another fast-moving cloud rushed through the air.

Barne ran for his life, dropping the sphere.

The cloud stretched out, almost like a point, and came right for him. He looked over his shoulder as it flew past him and into another warrior he hadn't noticed was there.

This time, he saw exactly what happened. Every part of the warrior, even his clothing and weapons, dematerialized into vapor, except something round from inside his chest. Gravity pulled the sphere to the earth, where it instantly started to harden.

Barne turned every which way, wondering why the cloud wasn't going after him, why it had spared him and not the others? Or maybe he was next.

"Oh, no. What have I done?" He put both hands on his face as he realized that he was responsible for two deaths. Now he understood the true importance of rules—sometimes when you break them, they break you in return.

# Here I Come

~Valara~

Valara heard the news of her son's treachery during her shift change.

The gatherers weren't fully asleep yet—still snickering about the event as if he were an object or something completely devoid of feelings, thoughts and emotions. This gave Valara the drive she needed to do what would follow.

"I need more time," she said, pacing back and forth.

Giving up on being covert, she went straight to her tunnel, which was getting close to being completed. She immediately started to chip and dig at the hard surface. There was no time to be quiet or grind the large rocks into dust, or even dispose of the evidence.

"Faster! You're going too slow," her hand berated her.

"I'm going as fast as I can."

"Let me do it," the hand grabbed a second jagged rock.

Now, with both hands working in tandem, rubble fell at her feet as a testament of her strength.

"What's going on down there?" a voice echoed down the narrow tunnel. She had been careless, and didn't even cover the entrance.

Appearing defeated, she dropped her rocks and hung her head. "I got lost."

"What is this place? Who else is down here?" The silhouette of a man stood in the tunnel.

"No one else is here," her hand said, as it went for his throat, biting it out. He gurgled and wheezed, until its words became true. After years of digging, grinding and destroying her insides, her plan was about to come to fruition. One thing was for damn sure, she was getting out of there tonight, and nothing was going to stop her.

# Nature's Rule



After days of interrogation and torture, Barne had finally reached the end of his line. Today was his trial and execution. It wasn't a matter of "if" they were going to kill him; it was more a matter of "how" they were going to do it. He had broken sacred rules, and the forest had to see order restored; that is what they told him, anyway. Two folk were gone because of him, and he wanted to be punished in order to rid himself of the guilt that ate away at him like a plague.

He was stuffed inside a giant spiked tuber, and any attempt to escape would most likely end in impalement.

"It's time, filth!" said a guard, whose fists Barne had gotten to know quite well as of late.

Someone lowered down a thick vine. Barne wrapped it around his waist and was raised out of his confinement.

Barne was led to an underground tree that grew from the ceiling like a stalagmite. Never had he seen something so extraordinary, yet so fitting. Its leaves were thin like a spider's web, and it swayed back and forth as if a wind forced it, though down here, none existed.

They laid him under the tree's hanging leaves, on a rock that naturally resembled a person. The cold rock soothed his nerves. It was almost peaceful gazing upon the hanging tree above him. He imagined himself a bird, looking down at the world from the great blue ocean in the sky.

He waited for the judge to sentence him, though none came. Instead, everyone he had ever met lined up for his procession.

First, he was met by one of the kids that he used to play the "Out of Sight" game with. A while back, he had earned himself a name, yet Barne had never learned it.

"Idle," he said and stabbed a double-sided quill into Barne's arm. It caused an intense pain for such a small weapon. He felt comfort in the sting as it tore through his flesh.

"When?" Barne winced.

Before Barne could get a response, he was gone.

Next, the little kid who had witnessed him escape towered over him. "Coward," he said, and stabbed him in the toe with a quill.

Barne tried to wiggle his toe, but it felt detached, as if it were frozen.

The third visitor was another kid he had spent years with. Barne tried to quickly search his memories to guess what transgressions he had committed against the girl, though he couldn't think of anything. The girl's hands shook as she picked up a striped quill, scouring his body for the perfect spot to punish.

"What have I done to you?"

"Play," the kid said, as she jammed the needle into Barne's knee, creating a multitude of uniquely painful sensations.

Barne's breath shuttered as he exhaled.

A round-looking folk towered above him with a smirk.

Barne was positive that he'd never seen him before.

"Glutton," Merim said, jamming a quill inside Barne's stomach.

Then he was met by his old friend, Seyu.

A smile half-heartedley came to Barne's mouth. "Seyu," he stammered.

Like a ghost, his emotionless expression looked onward. "False names...consuming insects," Seyu said, picking up two needles and stabbing one into each of Barne's lips. His friend had betrayed him, like he said he never would. Everyone had a price, and Barne was paying for all of them.

One by one, other members of the tribe came to dole out his punishment. They truly believed that he was a spy, sent here to unbalance their way of life. No one would have ever expected a child, so they thought. Paranoia and speculation became rampant, like a disease. Everyone blamed their problems on Barne, whether it made sense or not. He had hundreds of quills sticking out of him like a porcupine. He tried to move, but his body was paralyzed. All he could do was think of the two warriors who had turned into mist before him, and he felt at peace with his end.

A delicate leaf floated down from the tree above like a feather. Barne could almost hear music playing as it sparkled from the cool light of the glowstones inside the chamber. The leaf landed directly on his body, now nearly covered with needles. It was then that Barne realized who was really passing his judgment. It was the hanging tree.

Barne realized he wasn't imagining the music. It was his favorite song, being sung from the lips of his friends. They were saying goodbye in their own way. Barne thought about how he had never learned to join them in song.

Nanis was the last of the long line of people inflicting his sentence. Each betrayal hurt emotionally as much as the quills hurt physically. The closer he was to someone, the more pain it caused him on both fronts, almost like they were connected somehow. Nanis was his mentor, almost like a father to him, and he feared his sting would hurt most of all.

"I am truly sorry, old friend. You were like my own." He picked up the final quill-needle, which was much larger than the rest. Nanis held the power to end him in a single blow.

Barne could see the hesitation in his tired eyes as they shifted back and forth, looking for another solution. Stretching out his neck, Nanis debated taking his own life so that he wouldn't have to take that of another...someone he truly cared about; maybe the only person he ever did.

Barne communicated the only way he could—by shedding a tear. He wanted to let his mentor know that it was going to be all right. Barne felt that he was already dead, and at this point he wanted it to end more than he wanted to live.

Seeing Barne's grief, Nanis snapped out of his inner turmoil. He understood that his friend forgave him for what he had to do.

"Half-breed," Nanis said raising the quill in his hand. Barne finally knew the word he had been trying to define his whole life...half-breed. That was the secret kept even from himself—why he had to wear the hat and all the other strange things, why he never felt like he belonged or fit in, why he was met with opposition at every turn—because he was different. He didn't belong, and he was never going to. All he wanted was to be happy, even if it was fleeting. He wanted the pain to end, and death was going to give him his wish; so he hoped.

This was the end of him. All he had sacrificed for the tribe was forgotten over some petty mistakes. He thought about the one face that he didn't ge --------

Nanis stabbed the quill-needle straight into his brain, and Barne left this world just as he had entered it...with shame.

# Hardened by Stone

~Valara~

Valara broke through the wall that had stood as a monumental obstacle for longer than she cared to remember. Defeating the rock was all she had desired. Finally, she had done the impossible.

Looking through the crack linking her current life with her past, she couldn't help but smile upon smelling the halls of her former life. It brought momentary peace to her. She all but forgot the reason for her hardship in the first place..."Barnacle."

She slammed her body into the crack over and over again, knowing no fear, pain or defeat. The earth crumbled against her fortitude, until an avalanche of rocks fell, knocking her to the ground.

"No, no!"

Her feet were buried in collapsed rocks. She didn't have enough strength to reach the boulders to free herself. She had come so far and suffered so much, and now that she was on the cusp of victory, she was trapped.

Profanities escaped her mouth freely as she struggled, catching the attention of a passerby.

"Calm down. Are you okay?" the female asked, thinking this was a standard cave-in.

Valara tried to hide her face with her hand, but she had no way of hiding her hand.

"Get these rocks off me before I bite your face off," the hand challenged.

"Valara?"

Hearing her own name brought a moment of clarity to her mind.

"Yes," she admitted.

"It's me."

Valara covered one hand over the other one, hiding her "friend."

The woman gently touched Valara's face, guiding it to look upon her. The darkness masked most of the woman's features, though there *was* something familiar about her, something almost friendly.

"It's me—Bae."

Bae had been her third trustworthy companion. She hadn't seen her since the night of the conception. Knowing that her other two "trusty" colleagues proved less than loyal (since one had extorted her for food and the other had helped to de-throne her), to say that she wasn't exactly feeling hopeful would be an understatement.

Without hesitation, Bae began tossing the smaller rocks off of the pile that confined Valara.

"This big one has to go. Pull when I say," Bae instructed, digging out around the largest of the rocks.

They started to work together, just like old times.

"She's going to kill us," the hand said, infesting her with doubt.

"What was that?" Bae asked, catching her breath.

"Nothing. I'm ready," Valara said, grabbing onto a root that was jutting out of the wall behind her.

Bae pressed her back against the opposing wall and positioned her feet on the rock. "Go!"

Using their combined might, the boulder shifted enough to allow Valara to pull her legs out from under it. Doing so caused the whole pile of rocks to tumble, and Bae along with them.

Valara took to her feet, holding a rock inside her mouth-hand. Thoughts of murder and deception were beginning to form.

"Wait, I can help you...I just helped you. What I mean to say is, I can help you more," Bae reasoned, seeing Valara's evil stare.

Her hand spoke of death, but she couldn't hear it due to the rock in its mouth.

Letting the rock fall to her side, Valara extended her arm, choosing kindness over hatred.

Bae accepted her gesture and greeted her old friend with a warm embrace.

"Why are you here? I thought they expelled you to the outer camps."

"They did, but I escaped, to save my..." she couldn't bring herself to finish the sentence.

"Oh, my, that started hours ago."

"Where? I have to save him, take him away from here," Valara toppled over her words, releasing herself from Bae's arms.

"The hanging tree."

Valara started limping her way down the corridor.

"No, no, this way." Hand in hand, Bae led them through the twisting tunnels, which curved like intersecting veins.

"Where is everyone?" Valara asked, stumbling on the uneven ground.

Bae caught her before she met the ground with her face.

"At the sentencing, I presume."

"Why are you not there?"

"I have no ill will toward him." Bae made sure Valara was steady before continuing their journey.

"It looks as though you're the only one," Valara scoffed, seeing a long line of folk leaving the event.

They knew it would be nearly impossible to slip in unnoticed.

"What are we going to do? They're killing him," Valara said.

"Kill them all," the hand demanded.

"What? Wait here. I will handle it," Bae said, rounding the corner.

Valara sat, watching, twitching, as her last loyal subject approached the people responsible for causing harm to her "everything."

Valara's hand was always quick to speak the words she thought but feared to admit. "She's going to turn on you, like everyone else has."

"Stop it. I trust her."

"I trust no one."

"That's where we differ. I trust you," she confessed.

"You shouldn't. I tried to kill you, remember?" the hand admitted.

"No, it was the other way around."

"Was it?"

"Shhh!" Valara said, as she monitored Bae's body language while she talked to someone in the crowd.

"We have to go. She's taking too long!" The hand grew impatient.

Before Bae had a chance to create a diversion, she noticed Valara darting toward the crowd. The folk she was talking to saw it too— the fear in his eyes betrayed him.

"Don't call me such things!" Bae came up with a different diversion, as she palmed the man's mouth and took him to the ground. She hoped he was the only one to bear witness to Valara's presence.

The crowd directed their attention toward Bae awkwardly wrestling the folk on the ground.

Valara limped into the room. With each step, a crunching noise echoed through the hall and was accompanied by a sensation which mirrored its sound, but she didn't even notice. She approached the hanging tree and slowed down, making certain that the area was empty.

On the sacrificial stone, there lay a part of her, the part she wished she could have kept for herself. The part that was viciously removed from her.

Valara rushed to him, tripping over herself. A trail of tears streaked her cheeks; some stemmed from merriment, but most were sorrow.

She had given everything she had, and still she was too late...

Finding an open spot between the slender, needle-like quills, she gave him a heartfelt kiss.

He looked so sad and disappointed, yet so grown and beautiful. He had surpassed her in size and bulk. How she wished she'd been able to spend every second watching him grow and sprout into what lay before her.

She slid her arms under his back, finding an area void of sharp points.

He was hers again, and she was taking him home with her.

Valara slowly carried his limp body out of the chamber, without a plan, without a care. Every time she stepped, some quills scratched against her body. Yet nothing slowed her stride.

The diversion didn't prove to last very long. They soon saw through Bae's ploy, and everyone was afoot, looking for the fugitive.

Valara wasn't hiding, merely walking at a crawling pace. Still, no one could find her. They rushed up and down the subterranean tunnels, never seeing the obvious. Maybe it was the will of the forest or her uncaring disposition, or maybe it was something as simple as chance, but it seemed almost as if she were invisible.

She reached the topside and walked right past the guard post just as the guard turned his head, scouting in the opposite direction. With her grown child in her adoring arms, and a lame foot dragging, she was free.

Valara's will was powered by adrenaline alone. Her muscles and bones had been spent long ago. She continued on, heading straight for the Flower Grove, to the very spot where she had brought him into this world. It was where she had found love, and it would be their final resting place. It was the only place in this world worthy of his smile.

They were close to the grove. She could feel its powerful presence, though she knew that she couldn't make it there. Smelling the sweet aroma of flower pollen, she fell to one knee. She knew he couldn't indulge in the fragrance, not now, not ever again.

She tried with everything she had left to return to her feet but fell over instead. She was depleted; this place would have to suffice. She had always wanted to share its magic with him, as he had shared his with her.

Valara clawed the ground with her fingers, dragging her arm into a position to cradle her child one last time.

"I cherish the time we had, if only brief. My prince, you are without...equal." She closed her eyes as flower petals dusted their intertwined bodies.

# Fresh Breath

~Barne~


------t to see.

arne opened his eyes, screaming from the agonizing pain. With his vision blurred, all he could make out was the large quill-needle that had just been pulled out of his head. It was still half-covered in blood—his blood.

He moved his hand to cover the gaping hole it had made.

"What are you doing? You're supposed to be dead!" The woman reacted loudly, dropping the needle on the ground.

"Grrrnaammn," Barne tried to talk, but it came out all mixed together.

She approached the living corpse slowly, trying to make sense out of everything.

Barne noticed something was attached to him. He flinched, and it crumbled around him like rotted wood.

"Shhh, don't move," the woman said. She was trying to conceive of the impossible. Had Barne survived his own execution? Or had he somehow turned undead? Knowing that the less alive were mindless, she figured a simple test was in order. "I am going to put this spike back inside your brain, okay?"

Barne snarled and kicked at her.

She couldn't help but jump back a full five feet.

He understood her. That meant only one thing—he *was* alive.

"Okay, okay. No more pain, I promise."

"Move?" Barne grunted, much clearer than before.

"You still have more quills stuck inside you. I can remove them, but I need you to be still. Can you do that for me?"

He didn't answer this time. His labored breathing was the only indication that he was still with her.

The woman picked up the tool that she had perfected for such a task. It was two flat rocks teetering on a twig and secured with plant husks. She had been removing quill-needles for about an hour before Barne had mysteriously come back to life.

Barne let out a whimper as she pulled out quill after quill, dropping them on the bed of needles she had removed previously.

"Where am I?" Barne finally managed.

"Valara rescued you...from judgment."

"How?"

"I don't know exactly. It was over a year ago."

"Impossible. Where is she? I want to see her face. Ow."

She had stumbled upon them by happenstance while making her yearly visit to the grove. Somehow fate decided she take a scenic route this time, and that is when she found them nestled together like an endless dream.

Barne and Valara had both been lost to the tribe for quite some time now. Many expeditions had searched the forest to no avail.

"I don't think she made it."

"What do you mean?"

She ignored the question, fearing her own sadness. "Last one. This might hurt a bit."

He saw the woman's tool close up as she brought it toward his left eye. In one swift motion, she pulled the final needle out. Blood trailed behind, dripping on his face.

Void of the crippling effects of the needles, Barne was free to control his body once again.

Wiping his face, his vision was now clear, as if the wound had never existed. In fact, none of his wounds were bleeding; they were just open holes.

He looked at the woman who had saved him. A large scar across the center of her face made her look experienced. He didn't remember ever making her acquaintance before, though she seemed to know him well.

"Who are you?"

"I'm Bae. I was a friend of your mother's."

"Where is her body?" Barne asked eagerly.

Bae crouched down next to him, as he clenched his teeth with worry. She dusted the husk that lay near his feet and pulled out a sphere similar to the ones he had found in the forest before he was caught.

"I've seen those. What is it for?"

"You don't know what this is? What you are?"

Barne looked at her blankly.

"This is your mother. What's left of her, anyway."

Barne held out his trembling hand, and she placed the orb inside it. Upon further inspection, the sphere looked a lot like a seed of some kind.

"It's the core of a feathered-folk, the pit. The only part of us that can never really die."

"So, we can bring her back?" Barne tightened his grasp around the seed, hope in his eyes.

"I'm afraid not."

"I miss her so much."

"I know...I know. It just doesn't work that way."

He contemplated life and death, and wondered if this was what was destined to come.

"Do I have one?"

"Humans have a soft organ called a heart. You..."

"I'm not human," he interrupted brashly. Barne knew the stories of the humans, and that all the tribe's hardships were caused by the fleshy horrors.

"You're as much human as you are folk," Bae blurted out.

"It's true, then? I'm a..." he started to say, disgusted.

"...half-breed, yes. You have the core of a folk, though the blood of a human."

"How did this happen?"

"It was a long time ago. I don't want to remember it."

"You mean...you were there?"

"No one should have been. I can't speak of it," Bae said, looking back in the direction of the human castle.

"How is it that I'm still alive and she..." Barne asked, looking at the pit he cradled inside his hands.

"I have never seen such wizardry. The forest is not done with you yet.

"Lucky me," Barne said, thinking about how very drab his life had been.

"It isn't luck. It's a blessing."

"What am I to do with myself?" Barne asked, trying to stand. "Everything I do ends up in pain and sorrow."

Bae walked over to help him, though he waved her away.

"Survive, which means staying away from your kind."

"Which ones, folk or human?"

"Both are equally dangerous. I suggest you leave the forest. Find a city or town. Leave this place and never look back. Forget what you know. Forget everything," Bae said, sprinkling some dust upon the pile of needles, disintegrating them instantly.

"I thought the folk could never leave the forest?"

"That's correct, but you're different. You're evolved," Bae said, wishing she could someday join him outside this place.

"Can you tell me who he is? My father, that is."

"The lord of the human castle—a vicious, cruel, evil thing. Need I say more?" She tossed him a small satchel. It was the only thing she had to give him that might prove useful during his long journey.

Barne shoved the pit inside the bag.

Bae turned her back to him, pausing to gather her words. "She loved you...and died for you. I can't say someone would do as much for me." When Bae spoke of his mother, the small buds on top of her head started to bloom into glorious flowers. Never had he seen a more magical sight. It was then that he understood the drawback to being a half-breed. He ran his hands along the top of his head. That was why Nanis had made him wear a coif all those years.

"Take care," Bae said as she disappeared into the forest.

This time he saw the surface world much differently. It was so alive; everything was moving. Each leaf made its own sound as it talked to the steady breeze. His eyes couldn't focus on everything. It was all so...beautiful.

He drew the sweet aroma that filled the air deep into his lungs. Instantly, he felt as if his past was cleansed from him by the warm breeze.

Looking up at the passing world, the frightened actions of a winged beast alerted him to impending danger. Startled, he jumped back, as old bones, sharpened into spikes, fell upon the place he had stood moments before.

Barne had planned on taking Bae's advice to heart. He had spent many days trying to figure out which way was out. If a trap was here, he knew that he must still be inside their territory. Barne moved in the opposite direction, thinking that traps were set to guard the perimeter.

He didn't know if it was the echo of his own footsteps, the rustling of the leaves, or if someone was dangerously close behind him. His curiosity didn't cause him to falter. He tried to breathe shallowly and move steadily, not letting his fear take over—resulting in a careless mistake.

Sure enough, he was being stalked by a warrior of the woods not too far away, though he remained out of sight.

Barne glided swiftly and accurately. Keeping his eyes on the terrain ahead that kept him from making a misstep. Fixating his eyes on the ground had one major drawback, however...he ran directly into a stone wall.

The world was spinning around him as he staggered as if intoxicated.

He saw a figure approach him, with an outstretched hand.

Instead of facing him, Barne turned and scaled the stone wall. He rolled over the top, splashing into a large stream.

He had no reason to believe anything but the ground was going to catch his fall.

The cold water shocked his system as he struggled to maneuver in the watery effusion.

Flailing and splashing, he swallowed a mass of the liquid as the stream swept him away. His body tried valiantly to cough up the choking water. The raging torrent turned him around, constantly pulling at his legs. He was getting destroyed out here.

He managed to wrap both his hands around a rock jutting out from the center of the river. There were scaly beasts flying through the current underneath him. They were magically graceful.

He took a long while to regain his composure and devised a plan to escape this trap.

Though the rock was slick with algae, he managed to climb on top of it, keeping his body low like a frog.

Watching the fish, Barne began to learn through observation and mimic their movements.

Once he was ready, he jumped into the water and tried to reach the shore. This was slightly more effective than what his instincts told him to do, but it wasn't enough to keep him afloat.

His head bumped against a shallow rock, and his body became limp.

Knocked out, he floated downstream. Luckily, his head was face up, still providing him oxygen. Ironically, he was much better now than when he was conscious.

Only out for a couple of moments, his eyes fluttered open. He felt weightless and free. He feared that if he moved, it would be ruined.

Approaching a calm pool, he slowly drifted to the edge—as fate had decided.

Pulling himself out of the water, he had developed a new love and hatred for streams. It was just one of the splendors that the surface had to offer. Maybe at another day and time, he would be able to perfect his dance with the wild mistress.

It didn't take long for the heat of the sun to evaporate all the water drops off him. His clothes felt tighter than before.

He heard a loud banging that appeared to be getting closer. Irritated, he wanted to run away from it. Instead, he followed its deafening ring.

Near a tamer offshoot of the stream stood a small straw-roofed hut. Barne had never seen an above- ground dwelling before. He looked at it inquisitively as it appeared odd by all accounts.

He figured it could possibly be the residence of an evil human. Although, on second thought, it looked much too small for such a creature, based on their reputation.

The sound, however, matched what he could only imagine was the crashing stride of the nefarious metalmen he had heard about. It was almost upon him, making him feel jittery and cold.

He hid adjacent to a thorny bush, and waited.

Finally, the source of the horrific sound came into view. It was a small man, smaller in size than even he was. Inside each of his hands, he held a shiny metal disc which he banged against the other.

Puzzled by its smallness, Barne wondered if this could be a human child. *He's wrinkly and his hair is old. It can't be.*

No longer scared of the humanoid, Barne made his presence known. "Greetings."

The man stood frozen in place, no longer making his musical disaster.

"Are you a human?"

Crash! The man banged the discs together once more.

Barne winced. The sound was much worse close up. "Can you please..."

Crash!

This time the ringing noise bounced around inside Barne's head, instantly giving him a headache. "...stop that!"

The human made a motion to strike the two discs again, though he stopped an inch before they touched.

"Thank you," Barne said, still covering his ears.

The human dropped the discs on the stone path, creating a loud sibilance, as he fled the confrontation. He ran inside the stone-bottom, grass-top house, slamming the door behind him.

Barne didn't know why, but he chased the figure, nearly missing his nose getting caught on the closing door. "I just want to talk to you," Barne yelled, banging on the wooden door. "Come on!"

Soon he gave up on having a friendly encounter with the man.

Barne wondered how humans managed to find so many perfectly square-shaped stones to accommodate the house design. As he felt the strength of the stonework, it looked more visually stunning than practical.

"You put all these strong stones on the bottom and weak grass on the top. I don't even think it would hold my weight," Barne couldn't help pointing out.

To prove his point further, he picked up a medium rock and rested it upon his chest. Crouching down, he heaved the rock into the air. It crashed right through the roof of the hut, making a huge hole.

As fast as the rock went into the hut, the man came out, directly into the waiting arms of Barne.

"Shhh," Barne tried to calm him down.

Once the man knew that he couldn't wiggle his way out of the feathered-folk's superior grip, he gave up. Fear clouded his eyes.

"Do you understand me?" Barne asked.

The man didn't answer.

It wasn't clear whether the man spoke a different dialect or if he was deaf from all the banging. In either case, Barne had to find some means to communicate.

Upon touching the human, Barne finally understood where he got the softness to his bark-like skin. His hair, too, held a familiarity that was uncanny.

Barne quickly released his grip, liberating the man. He held both his hands high, surrendering his dominance. "You're free."

The man instantly began to crawl away. Then he paused, turning back to reclaim his loud smashers from the ground.

"Go ahead," Barne said with a nod.

The man smiled, picked up his discs and carried on like before, as if nothing had transpired.

Barne covered his ears, perplexed by his first encounter with the other half of himself. He wondered if they were really as bad as he had been told. But they were definitely louder.

As the man marched away, the discord faded to a distant buzz. Barne took it upon himself to enter the human house. Metal tools and knickknacks were shoved in any open spot.

He tossed his satchel into a pile.

It was strange how it just blended in, like it belonged there, mingling with the rest of the junk.

Figuring that he would hear the human returning from a safe distance, he laid his head down on the soft, fur-lined bed. He thought he'd try to catch some sleep like a human. For the first time in his life, he felt civilized...and comfortable.

# False King

## ~Hoger~

Hoger sat tall on his righteous throne, wondering why everything had been falling apart around him. An adviser was going over details regarding the folk/human sanctions.

"We cannot just abandon that part of the forest. Its resources are much too valuable," the adviser explained, peering over a hand-drawn map.

"They have the upper hand. And we need to break that hand," Hoger said, The Pit of the Forest—the feather-folks' most prized jewel—clasped inside his palm.

"They have already built a wall around our water supply!" the adviser said, while wrinkling the map with his over-exaggerated gesticulations.

"Watch your tone."

"Sorry for the intrusion, sir." An out-of-breath warrior burst into the royal chamber.

"Not now," Hoger said with a snap of his fingers.

"But...I've found them..."

"Valara?"

The warrior now had Hoger's full attention.

Still without a solution to his current predicament, the agitated adviser leaned against a wall, looking defeated. He feared that Hoger was never going to seriously heed any of his advice.

"Yes. A couple hours east of the grove."

"Did you capture them?"

"Well...no. They went over the wall before I..."

Without warning, Hoger threw whatever was inside his hand at the warrior. This time it happened to be the precious artifact.

Violent outbursts were a somewhat normal occurrence with the reactionary leader.

The warrior dodged out of the line of fire, mostly out of habit.

A guard approached the warrior, his mouth twisted in disgust. "Defending yourself against your chieftain is like attacking him directly," the guard scolded, kicking the warrior to his knees.

The adviser rushed over and picked up the artifact carefully, showing it the precious treatment it deserved. "Sir?"

"Uh, I know I shouldn't have thrown it. It's his fault for upsetting me."

"It's not that."

"Can you just stop bugging me for one single day? Then maybe, just maybe, I might actually be able to get rid of this headache," Hoger grumbled.

"I think I know why things are so bad for us."

"Can it wait until I'm finished with this incompetence?!" Hoger gestured at the warrior.

"No!" the adviser yelled through years of pent-up frustration. He was sick of being an adviser who couldn't advise, simply because his leader was too bull-headed to listen.

The guard approached him with a raised arm.

"It's fake. Look at the crack," the adviser said, edging toward Hoger and away from the guard.

"Let me see," Hoger snatched the jewel from his hand. "Colored glass," he concluded, as black sand leaked out of the center of the counterfeit gem. "She must have the real one. Send everything we've got over the wall, if you have to."

The adviser smiled deeply. For the first time in a long time, his advice was being taken into account.

# The Deep

~Barne~

arne woke up abruptly, not to the crashing sound of the human, but to the marching drum of war. His people were on the move. That meant only one thing—they had found him.

He rushed over to the stream to rejuvenate himself for the long journey ahead. The water was cold and refreshing, tasting alive.

Out of the corner of his eye, he spotted something floating downstream. Bobbing up and down, it was caught in the current. Thinking nothing of it, he continued to lap up water, letting it spill all over his clothes.

A few more items raced by, this time in a pack. Again, Barne tried to make out what they were. Taking in one last gulp from the stream, he finally recognized them.

"Pits..." He spat out the last of his mouthful and took to the forest.

His people were dying upstream, and he had an idea as to what was doing the killing—a force that he couldn't beat, nor did he want to try.

After running for what seemed like hours, he eventually came upon a stone tower that peered over even the tallest of trees. Mesmerized, Barne didn't know if it was constructed to show its dominance over the forest, or simply as a beacon to disclose its location.

Normally Barne would have run as far away from this monolithic marvel as possible, but after meeting a real human, he didn't find them at all terrifying. Maybe this castle would shed some insight on his place in this world. Or perhaps this was the very same castle Bae had spoken of.

He lived his whole life in a hidden village, where each entryway was carefully concealed between trees, leaving access only to those with the know-how to find them.

Humans, on the other hand, had a very intriguing, *here I am, so deal with it,* type approach.

Barne walked along the human trail paved in stone. He couldn't miss the many signs and arrows posted everywhere, even if he tried. Barne started to get the idea that humans had no sense of direction.

Many twists and intersections later, he was nearly at the foot of the castle. He found it quite odd that not a single human was outside.

"Castle Deep," Barne read the sign posted in front of the archway.

*How come I can read it?* He wondered if the sign was written as a warning to the folk or if they shared the same dialect.

*How do the humans ever enter the castle walls?* He thought maybe an invitation was required.

He walked closer to the castle. Smoke encircled the monstrosity. He smelled fire and instantly felt the need to take to the underground.

Resisting the urge, he decided to have a closer look. Surrounding the castle lay a deep ravine. It was filled with smoldering trees which had been cut and quartered. *It all seems so foreign.* He couldn't figure out the purpose of any of it.

Without warning, a blast of fire erupted out of the ravine, knocking him off his feet. Ash and soot marred the walls, as the heat forced him backwards.

The raging fire rippled like a stream and circumscribed the entirety of the castle.

He *really* started to wonder how they got in now. What humans lacked in physical prowess, they more than made up for with their ingenuity.

He wondered if the fire was set ablaze just for him. *They know I'm only one person, right?*

Barne causally sauntered away from the impenetrable castle, thinking he wasn't at all welcome.

That's when he got his invitation, from an arrow as it stabbed him through the back.

Not feeling the sharp pain right away, Barne touched the point sticking out of his chest before collapsing.

***

Freezing cold water washed away Barne's slumber. He was chained to a stone wall. The stones were colder than the water. Still shivering from the shock, another bucket came at him with little warning, hitting him directly in the face.

"I'm awake!"

"It can speak..." the bucket man said, with a raised eyebrow.

Unable to wipe his face, Barne used his breath to blow the constant dripping off the tip of his nose. "I've come peacefully. I only wish to gain entry to your fine castle."

"Congratulations, you're already here," the man said, stacking his wooden buckets inside each other. With an uninterested shrug, he left the damp room.

Cold light from the moon illuminated the smoke outside through a small arrow slit. He knew he was drawn to this place for some reason, and now that he was here, he didn't know what he had expected exactly, but this wasn't it.

Before long, he was met by a stout man decorated in shiny garments, which were most likely human metal. He had deep lines on his expressionless face—evidence that he had, at one time, showed emotion. He was accompanied by an armed guard.

"Greetings, feather-man. I am Lord Neff, the commandant of this castle."

Barne wondered if this could be him—his father. He froze at the very notion.

"Why are you here? I once gave your people a message. Or was I not clear?" the lord continued.

"I came to see you," Barne said, finding his voice.

"What business could you possibly have with me? Please, indulge me."

Barne wanted to tell him about his mother, and that he was his own blood. He imagined them sharing a warm embrace and living in harmony. Maybe the lord would be convinced that the forest could be shared by both their kind living equally. He soon realized that was just a dream when...

"Spit it out, boy!" the guard ordered, accompanied by a metal-handed slap.

"Peace. I've come for peace."

"Really? Have you? Then why do you break our truce?

"I don't follow."

"By coming here, you have raised a banner of war," Neff said, stroking his stubble. "Kill him. Send a message of war back to those feathery folks."

The guard happily drew his longsword. Barne noticed that his eyes didn't blink at the same time; one was slightly slower than the other.

"Wait..."

"I don't think you're in any position to make demands."

"I'm not a feathered-folk..."

The guard let out a huge amount of laughter, lowering his sword.

"...I'm a half-breed. I'm your son."

Without missing a beat, the guard hit Barne over the head with the hilt of his sword, knocking him out cold.

# How the Other Half Lives



Barne's head ached as he awoke inside a human bed twice the size of the one he had slept in previously. The bedding was scratchy and warm. He ran his hand over his head and felt a tender lump where he had been struck.

"Sorry for the intrusion," a female voice said.

Barne sat up, noticing that he had been washed and dressed in the human's customary garb.

"I'm...not in prison," he reluctantly said.

The well-groomed human woman brought over a tole filled with cheese and meats. Barne knew that such foods were forbidden among his people, but he was no longer among them, was he?

Barne dove in with both hands, rapidly shoveling the food inside his starved mouth. He jostled the tray, causing some scraps to spill out on the floor.

The woman placed the tray next to his legs and reached for the wasted pieces. "That's okay..." she started to say.

Barne snatched them out of her hand, scarfing them down before she was fully standing up again.

It had been a long time since he had remembered eating food. In truth, it was far longer than he had imagined.

The smell was intoxicating, the taste—sensational. Never had he experienced such flavors and textures! Everything was prepared to excite the palate, not for sustenance.

The woman hurried out of the room while Barne was licking the flavors off his fingertips.

When she returned, she held another platter, twice the size of the previous one.

He polished off this second course more slowly this time, savoring every bite. His stomach gave up before his taste buds did. Still, he forced himself to finish off the delightful treats.

"Shall I get another?"

"No, I don't think I could control myself if you did."

The woman left him with an endearing smile, taking both trays with her.

"Madam," Neff said, crossing her on his way into the chamber.

Barne couldn't hide his satisfied smile even if he had wanted to; and he did want to.

"Are you okay?" Neff asked with open arms.

Barne nodded, unsure if he should be answering.

"How is your head?"

Barne winced upon feeling the spot again, as if he was commanded to do so.

"Our family never did take too kindly to bumps," Neff said, placing both hands on Barne's shoulders, causing him to flinch. "I can see the resemblance."

Barne had never really seen himself, so he had to take the lord's word for it. He wondered if Neff was lying just to be hospitable. In any case, it was welcoming.

"This will be your kingdom someday. Better learn how to protect it. Come."

Barne took a beat, genuinely shocked by what he had just said. No one had ever treated him so well. He felt it might be a dream...or the afterlife.

"There is a big world out there, and it isn't going to rule itself," Neff said, already in the hallway.

Catching up, Barne followed the human like a shadow. He was met with strange looks from people as he passed by them in the drafty halls. No one looked at him like Neff did—with acceptance.

They entered an elaborate war room. Weaponry and metal suits of armor lined the walls. Barne wondered how many armaments they had, that they would have extra to act merely as decoration.

A pedestal stood at the end of a large table. Sitting on top, a cloth-covered object rested on a white pillow. Three roaring fireplaces kept the room toasty warm.

"Why are you treating me this way?" Barne blurted out.

"Believe it or not, you're not the first half-breed I have ever encountered."

"Really?"

"Of course. Where I come from, they are almost more common than humans," he said, putting a casual arm on the table.

Feeling intrigued by a much bigger world than this forest, Barne moved closer to the human.

Carved into the table was a map of the whole forest. It had hills, streams, and even a waterfall. There was so much of his homeland that he had never even explored.

"We are here," Neff said, making a gesture toward a wood-carved marker. It was pointy like a castle.

Barne picked it up off the table. "What great detail went into this."

"Yes, I had one of my finest artisans work on it. Careful, it's sharp."

Barne placed the castle marker back on the map, not wanting to damage it.

"So, where did you grow up?"

Barne looked around on the map, lost. "I'm not sure. I only ever ventured into the forest twice—this being one of them."

"Well, then." Neff clicked his heels, continuing on. "Upstairs we have the armory..."

"Lord?"

"Call me father."

"Uh...father, why are you showing me all this? Aren't you scared that I might give away all your secrets?

"I have nothing to hide. This is all mine, and soon yours. But those savages, they are not so transparent. They hide like little rats in a sewer, and just when you think they're gone, they bite you."

Barne couldn't help but feel offended, and it showed in how he shifted about.

"I don't mean you, of course, dear son. It wasn't your fault. They never told you about me, did they?" he asked, lifting a large decorative sword off the wall.

"Not exactly," Barne said while standing up straighter and far less casually.

"Have you ever seen one of these before?"

Barne shook his head.

Neff tossed him the heavy sword, which he dropped on the ground.

"See, you're royalty. Yet they hide your birthright. I get it. They hid it from me too, to torture and punish me. You see that, don't you?"

"I suppose," Barne said, distracted by the craftsmanship of the human blade. The edges were smooth and very sharp.

"Here, I want to show you something truly special." Neff approached the pedestal. Removing the cloth revealed a rich black gemstone which reflected all light against its perfectly cut edges. Neff carefully picked it up and it instantly came to life with swirling colors.

Soon images formed within the gem. They saw many feathered-folk climbing over the stone wall and attacking human soldiers.

"See how relentless they are? Invading us...and for what?"

"It's my fault. They're looking for me."

"Perhaps, perhaps not. What would they want with you?" Neff said with a twinkle in his eye.

They had already killed him once. Maybe they wanted to appease the forest and finish the job. Barne kept his thoughts to himself, not sure if he could trust the human yet.

"This is the only way to keep them at bay, and believe me, it pains me to do it," Neff said.

A robed figure with a cane hobbled toward Neff and started to chant loudly. His ancient-looking body generated a cloud-like substance between his hands.

Barne felt a biting terror wash over him as he recognized what was happening.

"It was you..." Barne said, starting to get flashbacks of the deaths he had witnessed in the forest. He was haunted, again seeing their faces turn into mist and fade away.

"When do you speak of?"

Neff held up the crystal, and the cloud went through the gem like a doorway to another place. Inside the gem, he could see the cloud crash into a feathered-folk, causing its body to be destroyed.

"I was there. Didn't you see me?" Barne said, confused.

"Of course I did."

"I have to know. Why did you take the warriors' lives and not mine?"

Neff was fixated on the gem, "You're my kin. I couldn't hurt you."

Barne knew that the lord didn't know they were related until he had told him, or else he wouldn't have put him in the torture room when he first arrived. Neff was lying about something, but Barne couldn't figure out what.

At the sight of the cloud, all the feathered-folk fled back over the wall.

"Look at those feathered-folk run," the cloud maker spoke out of turn, and met a cold stare from Neff.

"Well then, it's over," Neff said, returning the gem to the comfort of its pillow.

The cloud maker left the room in the same manner in which he came—slow and bored, his cane rattling.

"May I ask you something?" Barne said.

"Anything."

"Why do you call us feathered-folk?"

"Because it's what you are. Don't you call yourselves that?"

"Well...the thing is, despite looking like we do, we don't actually have any feathers—they're leaves."

Neff took a long, close look at Barne, seeing him in a new light. "So they are. Don't worry. I will make sure that from now on, we'll call you leaf-folk or whatever 'folk' you prefer."

"How about just 'people'?"

"Silly boy, *we're* people. You need a word to separate our kinds, if only for the ease of con-versation. Think about it and get back to me,"

Neff said, wiping his face on a white towel. "Is it hot in here?"

Barne thought the temperature was perfect, though all three fireplaces were still roaring. "Do you really want me to run things around here after you're gone?"

"Well...yes, of course. What I mean to say is, it may be a long while from now, but you definitely are my first choice."

"First choice?"

"If we're being completely honest with each other—and I hope we are—I must tell you that I have a couple of sons. They're far away, in a different castle. But rest assured, they are dullards and would have never been as brave or bold as you," Neff went on magnanimously.

Barne wondered if he was up to the task, or even willing to do it. "How many sons do you have?"

"Three...I mean four. I must not forget about you. Apologies. That could get some getting used to."

Barne pushed back his skepticism for the time being. Besides the bump on the head, Neff had been nothing but cordial and endearing. Maybe he could learn something from them after all.

"So, how can I help?" Barne asked, touching another marker on the map that resembled a claw.

"I am glad you asked. Look at how helpful you are." Neff cleared his throat, as if he had been waiting for Barne to prompt a speech he already had prepared for the occasion.

"I need you to go back to your homeland with a message: Leave the forest before the full moon returns or else I will burn it down. Every tree. Every bush."

"But...they can't."

"Why? Can't or won't? Did he say can't?" Neff said to the wall.

"Well...I..."

"He said 'can't', sire," an armored guard responded.

Barne was taken aback. Due to the stillness of the suit, he only assumed the guard was part of the decorations.

"What are they hiding? Tell me," Neff asked, getting uncomfortably close to Barne's face.

"They have nowhere else to go." Barne tried to cover his lie.

"I suppose, as an alternative, they can also surrender to me, and serve me in court. That wouldn't be so bad, right? I mean, look around. Isn't it lovely here?"

"What if they decline? Or worse...they could hurt me."

"They wouldn't do such a thing, would they? I am offering to let you go, completely un-scathed. Are they less merciful?"

"I suppose not," Barne said, shuttering as he thought about all the quills.

"Then it's settled. You shall depart at once...before they reassemble their forces," Neff said, clasping his hands together as if to congratulate himself.

Barne wasn't used to dealing with humans. Their kindness was overt and brash.

Before he knew it, castle staff had whisked him away, and he was outfitted with a travel pack and a generous amount of supplies for such a short journey. He didn't even get an opportunity to say goodbye to his father before departing for the very place he had fled.

Chains rattled and gears turned as the stone wall at the front of the castle lowered over the moat of fire, which had been reduced to embers. Barne finally knew how they entered and exited the castle, though he couldn't believe it was possible.

Barne was carried away by an animal-drawn transport to the border dividing their lands. The beast made strange but sweet noises.

A wooden bridge was pushed into place, making it easier for them to cross the stream. After reaching the other side, the bridge was removed.

Though the humans made good use of the wood they slayed, to him the trees were alive, and he found it rather peculiar to use their corpses in such a manner.

The loud sound of the transport's wheels alerted the whole forest to their presence. He imagined that if the wheels could speak, they were saying, "Here we are...right here...taking a ride in the forest. Better watch out."

While lazily watching the forest pass him by, he started to daydream about what a human city must be like. He couldn't even fathom what contraptions they were capable of creating. Their imagination seemed limitless.

All of a sudden he was snapped out of his dream-like state. Two golden eyes pierced his sense of security from the darkness of the dense forest ridge. They were looking at him deeper than merely sight could see. Barne covered himself with his hands while feeling rather uncomfortable. The eyes turned back into dark-ness, and he could have sworn he saw the silhouette of a large, cat-like beast.

A short while later, the transport stopped at the border of their lands. He knew this because of the wooden sign which told him exactly that.

He dismounted the transport without a word from the driver who sat above him.

Barne stood there, stuck exactly between both worlds, and he wanted nothing more than to get uninvolved with both of them. It was his pursuit of happiness that forced his legs back to the place he thought he had left behind forever.

# Homecoming

~Barne~

Through the mating call of the nightswift a voice interrupts the courtship. "We have the half-breed. We found him just outside the border," a warrior announced.

"Bring him in," Hoger commanded eagerly.

Barne stumbled in. His supplies had been confiscated and his fine human clothes torn. Barne could easily tell who had been at his execution by all the averted eyes as he entered the royal chamber.

"So, you've returned from the dead," Hoger said, with a chuckle. "Where's Valara?"

"She is gone."

"Search the forest. He's lying."

"No, I mean she's dead," Barne said, feeling a lump in his throat.

"Now you can join her."

"Hold on. I have a message for you from Lord Neff."

A synchronous gasp filled the chamber.

"I've heard his message before."

Warrior-folk gripped their weapons tightly, fearing this to be the beginning of the end.

"No, he swore it to me. He wants peace."

"His only desire is to destroy the whole forest, not just a piece."

"No, I mean, he no longer wants war."

"And if we refuse?" Hoger asked, resting his head against his hand.

"He said that you can either abandon the forest or work for him."

"You mean slaves?"

"No...for wages."

"Why would he send you, a despicable half-breed, with such an important message?"

"Because...I am...his son."

"What?!" Hoger erupted from his throne. Luckily for Barne, he had nothing to throw at that particular moment.

Lancer approached Hoger and whispered into his ear, confirming the assertion. Hoger growled loudly at her.

"You hid that from me? Your chieftain? Take her away—far, far, away."

Guards approached Lancer. She fought back with her twin swords, using surprise to her advantage. Four guards fell to the ground before some even readied their weapons. Outmatched and surrounded, she finally relinquished her weapons. She never gave up without taking a souvenir.

"Congratulations, you just weakened your people," Hoger said, through gritted teeth.

After Lancer had been escorted out, Hoger returned to his throne. "Kill the half-breed."

He picked up his "gem" and said a vulgar prayer to it just under his breath.

Barne had a guard on each side of him as they dragged him backwards, sliding him on his heels. "Neff, he has one of those in his war room."

Hoger's adviser put up a halting hand, stopping the guard mid-stride

Hoger gripped the false gem so tight that the crack splintered throughout it and sand ran down his arm.

"I've seen it. It shows him the forest from the trees' eye."

"No, you're wrong. He doesn't have *one* of these. He has *the* one. The Pit of the Forest," Hoger said, tossing his cracked imitation to the ground, shattering it. "How could I have not seen that?"

"I saw him use it...as a weapon."

"The reaping cloud," the adviser surmised.

"Yes, I saw his witchcraft. He conjured the thing out of thin air."

"Valara, her betrayal goes further than I thought. Her shame, it's everlasting. The boy, how can we use the boy?" Hoger mumbled to himself as his adviser approached.

"May I suggest?"

"Out with it already!"

"Send the half-breed to collect the artifact, then we will have the advantage. The boy knows the way; he got there unharmed."

"How is it you weren't obliterated by the reaping cloud?" Hoger pressed, looking up at Barne.

"I don't know. He said it was because I'm family."

"No, that's a lie."

"The Pit of the Forest can only see things of the forest. That's why we never saw the humans coming, and that's precisely why they didn't see *him* coming," Merim said, stepping forward.

"What do you know?" Hoger challenged.

"For years I've seen Valara use the artifact, and I know exactly what we should do with it once it's returned."

"Oh, you do?"

"Yes, I do."

"Why are you so chatty all of a sudden? This information might have proven useful when I was trying to get the FAKE ONE TO WORK!"

Merim was one of the three loyal officers who had known Valara's secret. For years, he had plotted and planned how he was going to overthrow Hoger. The only thing that had stood in his way was Lancer and her twin blades. Now that Hoger had locked her up, his opportunity had finally arrived.

"Even I couldn't have known it was false," Merim lied.

"Do you know why we dispose of half-breeds?" Hoger asked Barne, trying to calm himself down again.

"No."

"Because our whole existence is built off of traditions, and each half-breed dilutes those traditions. Just by breathing, you comprise everything we are..."

"I'm not trying to."

"...without even trying."

"I never asked for this."

"I know you didn't, but do you respect our traditions?"

"Of course."

"Then you must respect our tradition of killing all the half-breeds."

"But..." his adviser pleaded

"Make the arrangements," Hoger said.

***

Barne spent the next day going over everything in his mind. He could see that both sides had suffered immeasurably causalities, and refused to compromise their position. He was so deep in thought that he didn't notice he had a visitor.

"Hello, Barne," Nanis greeted him. "I have good news for you. Hoger has reconsidered his position. However, you will be banished from the forest forever if you fail to comply with his orders."

"Why?"

Nanis sighed deeply. "Sometimes he has trouble controlling his immediate reactions, but after seeking counsel, he realized you could serve a better purpose."

Barne wondered how such a knuckle-head had acquired the greatest position of power in the first place. Things were in upheaval around here, and it was abundantly clear that Hoger was to blame.

"Follow me. I have something to show you." Nanis led Barne through a tunnel near the surface—a forbidden area close to where he had grown up with the other children. Each guard they came in contact with was accommodating and granted them passage.

They arrived in a room similar to the one he had slept in, though it was much larger and filled with dirt mounds.

"The forest is rife with secrets. This one comes from the moonlight's rays," Nanis explained, taking careful steps to not disturb the mounds.

"What are they?"

"Younglings. Not like you, but pure, like me," Nanis said.

"I don't understand."

"I have a task for you, before going back."

"What kind of task?" Barne asked.

"We cannot die by normal means—not as long as this nursery exists. You, on the other hand, will die like a human does. Your heart cannot be reborn," Nanis continued, while pulling out the pit of a fallen folk and placing it in an open mound.

"Why are you telling me all this?"

"We need you to fetch as many fallen folk as you can. For the army."

Barne thought about his mother's pit; she could be resurrected. "What if I had Valara's pit? Could you save her here?"

"Do you have it?"

"I do...I mean did, but I left her back at Castle Deep."

"Her ancestry goes back farther than anyone else's. That was careless."

"They took all my belongings. Wait..." Barne thought about it for a moment. He hadn't had his satchel when he approached the castle. He last remembered having it...inside the grass hut! "I know where it is. It's safe...I think."

Nanis put a comforting hand on Barne's shoulder. "It would be very fortunate for a strong pit like hers to return to the tribe. I have to warn you, she *will* come back, but not as she once was—as someone new."

*Even if she comes back as someone else, something is better than nothing,* he thought to himself. "She brought me into this world. Now it's my turn to bring her back."

# Loose Ends

~Barne~


For the next couple weeks, Barne found himself commissioned with the quest of recovering fallen pits from the battlefields. Hoger wanted an army and he needed Barne to assemble the recruits, as he was invisible to the reaping cloud.

Barne started to understand his folk side more as he inspected the pits he gathered. Depending on how cracked they were, he could determine how old they were. Each had a unique color and texture that might be overlooked by the naked eye.

The whole camp was working hard to expand the nursery in preparation for the upcoming war.

The moon was nearly a sliver in the sky, when he was approached by Merim. "You were always a healthy eater," he said, standing behind Barne in the rations line.

"What do you mean by that?"

"Nothing. I have a job for you."

Barne wondered why everyone wanted to use him for their errands, like he was a piece of their property. "I'm busy enough collecting pits."

Merim forcefully pulled Barne out of line. "I wasn't asking for your opinion."

"What do you want?"

"Tomorrow, I need you to find the albino tree, and cut me off a piece of its bark. About this size," he instructed, stretching his hands about a foot apart. "Can you do that for me?"

"I suppose. What do I get out of it?"

"Your supper." Merim pushed back in line, taking Barne's rations along with his own—just like old times.

The next day, Barne had finished his sweep early, only having found three old pits. Since he had extra time, he decided to search for this "albino tree."

Because he had never seen such a tree, he decided to search an entirely new section of the forest—one that had never been part of a past conflict—and sure as rain, he found it.

The albino tree looked exotic and pure. Although, despite its color, it didn't look much different than the rest of the oaks.

Not one for questioning, Barne took out his digging spade and chiseled away at the bark. He took off a piece about the size Merim had instructed.

Clouds rolled overhead, making the forest dark and ominous.

He didn't know if it was a coincidence or his guilt imagining false signs. Nevertheless, he collected the bark and finished his daily quest, twice as hungry as normal.

Barne went straight to Merim's cleft, bark in hand, hoping to recover his rations from the previous night.

"Merim?" he called out.

No one answered.

It appeared he wasn't there. Through the window, he spied evidence that Merim had, in fact, already eaten both their meals.

"Figures."

He was about to leave when he heard a sound coming from inside the cleft. He rushed straight to the back of the room, hoping to find Merim...and he did. Merim was stuck to the wall, a stone sword pinning him there.

"Merim, are you okay?" Barne pulled the sword out of Merim's chest and caught him in his arms. His folk blood spilled on the floor.

"Hoger. He is..." He died in his arms, right then and there.

Barne took the weapon and dislodged Merim's pit from his body. Once removed, his body instantly turned into a husk.

He rushed it over to the nursery. "I found one more, Nanis," he said handing him the bright green pit.

"I thought you were..." Nanis stopped himself upon seeing it. "What happened?"

"I think Merim got on Hoger's bad side."

"No, I cannot accept this. Hoger is very specific about allowing his enemies to be reborn."

"You said they come back different?"

"Those are his rules. Not mine," he said, pushing the pit back at Barne.

"I want to save everyone. I'm not going to play favorites."

"Fine, you want to save him, you do it." Nanis went back to digging fresh holes.

Looking around the nursery, Barne watched a youngling crawl out of its mound for the first time. Covered in dirt, it looked soft and magnificent. Its cry immediately alerted a folk who swept up the babe in its arms.

Barne surreptitiously dropped Merim's pit into the mound and covered it, leaving a tiny hole for the moonlight to penetrate the pit.

*Good, now I can sleep tonight.*

Barne made his way back to Nanis. There must have been thousands of pits growing in the new nursery.

"I'm glad I didn't see where you put it. Merim and I didn't quite get along," Nanis admitted.

"I don't think he got along with anyone."

"I was going to ask you, how did you come across his body?"

"He wanted me to fetch him this..." Barne explained while taking out the white bark.

"Put that away! Where did you get that?"

"From the albino tree," he reluctantly said, shoving the bark back inside his pack.

"I know where it came from. Why do you have it?"

"Merim said…"

"Come with me," Nanis whispered, putting his arm around Barne as he led him to a quiet alcove.

"The albino is the first of all trees. It holds magical properties linked to each bloodline. And if Merim wanted it, then he was up to no good."

"Can I use it to help, somehow?"

"Absolutely not. It's forbidden to take from the white."

"But I already took from the white."

"Well, put it back."

Barne knew that Nanis was much more stressed than usual. Building this army was leaving him with very little time to sleep.

"I will take it back tomorrow."

Nanis let out a sigh, "That's a relief to hear. One thing…"

"Yeah?" Barne said, looking at the old folk's doleful face.

"I'm sorry about betraying you. I…"

"No, let's not do this right now. We all have done things we can't take back."

"Stop. Please, I need to say this."

"Okay."

"Call me selfish, but I couldn't live with myself after what I had done. Every night I contemplated taking my own life. The only thing that kept me alive was hoping someday...I could make it right by the forest and by you. Seeing you again made me feel as if the forest had granted my request. That's why I've been working so hard, to make right by you."

Without warning, Barne embraced his old friend as if he were still a little folkling. The feeling was the same—safe, warm and loving. "You've already made right by me, old friend...and then some."

# Seeing Yourself

~Barne~

That night, Barne tried to close his eyes and regain some energy, but the leaves kept calling him. He stood up, glancing at his dormitory mates who were fast asleep. Something was guiding him, shoving him from behind. It was the wind.

He couldn't resist its will as he stumbled over to his belongings. A large gust blew open his pack, and a twinkle of white caught his eye.

"Oh, it's you," he whispered.

A knife fell off a shelf and rolled next to his feet. Barne looked around, but no one was there.

All night long, Barne whittled and carved the wood as if something wanted to come out. Like an itch, he kept at it; feeling pleasure when he was on the right path and pain when he wasn't.

Soon it was finished, and he felt satisfied—even more so than eating the human's food.

He looked at his hands. They were bloodied from rubbing against the stone knife's handle. He tried to clean off the mask, but it was already stained.

Holding it up to get a better view, moonlight pierced through the eye holes of the sad-looking mask he had created. He couldn't resist any longer; Barne placed the mask upon his head. All he saw was darkness shrouding his sight.

Frightened, he pulled at the mask, but it didn't want to come off. Frantic, he took both hands and finally pried it off his face—tossing it across the room. He stared at the mask until he got up enough nerve to collect it. The wood felt hot to the touch. He placed it back in his pack and returned to bed.

Exhausted, he fell asleep the moment his head hit the ground.

In the morning, Barne was difficult to wake up. It took a whole barrage of children to break his connection with the dream world.

Even when he was awake, Barne felt heavy—dragging his feet as he walked. Folk spoke to him, but the words just bounced off. It was like the concepts were too obtuse and not coherent.

Barne picked up his bag, and the albino mask slid out like it had a mind of its own. Instantly he felt invigorated; everything was crisp and clear.

The mask called for his face again. He could barely resist the urge. He salivated at the mere thought of giving in. *No, this is not the time for such things.*

He suddenly remembered that he had a meeting with Hoger on this day and flew out of the room, no longer thinking of masks or other foolish notions.

Embarrassingly late, Barne bowed his head, showing his respect to a leader he didn't feel deserved it.

"What do you have to say for yourself, half-breed?" Hoger berated.

"I found as many as I could. We only need to stall the humans now."

"I was thinking more of an apology."

Barne had been working diligently to save their people, almost as though his life depended on it. He would give Hoger no such satisfaction for not being punctual.

"So, what do you want me to tell Neff?" Barne adjusted his clothes, which were still wrinkled from sleeping in them.

"Make sure the lord *believes* that we have left the forest. We will withdraw into the ground until our uprising."

"Remember the gem," the adviser chimed in.

"I was getting to that, you twit!"

Barne still didn't know how he felt about betraying his father. All he knew was that he had to comply with Hoger long enough to be released into the forest. This conflict needed to be resolved before everyone killed each other.

"Where was I? That's right, remember to steal the gem and return it to us," Hoger calmly said, almost treating Barne like a pure folk and not a useless half-breed.

"You know, you're asking me to lie," Barne said, forgetting his place.

"Would you rather die? Get him out of here before I change my mind."

Barne showed himself out of the chamber and went back to his dormitory. He was finally alone.

He couldn't wait to pull out the mask. It looked even more spectacular in the daylight. He placed it upon his head, and it held on to his face, like a hand.

His view faded into the background, and he saw another scene displayed over his own. It was somewhere else...it was back at the castle. He could hear the cracking of the fire moat.

"Where is that half-breed bastard, anyway?" Neff yelled to an empty room.

Barne realized that he was looking through his father's eyes. More importantly, he realized that Neff had never once asked him his name.

The lord looked right and left, then his demeanor changed. Neff stumbled over to the window ledge and slowly poured water into a flowerpot. "There you go."

Barne felt the feeling that Neff had for the plant. It caused him to rip the mask off his face again, which was much easier this time. *Was that...love?*

His final week was spent making preparations for his journey back to the humans. Most everyone had showed him some respect and gratitude for all his hard work. He felt important, like a hero. They seemed to want to spend time with him because of his differences, not despite them.

He was the oldest half-breed to ever walk the halls of their thousand-year-old village. Barne liked all the attention he was getting, though all he really wanted was to have some peace and quiet...alone with his mask.

During the day, he always managed to find a couple of free moments to spare, in order to spy on his father. He was considerate, caring and thoughtful—everything the half-breed had ever wanted to be, himself. He did feel dishonest watching him without consent, but he had learned so much about human compassion.

Today was his final day in the folk village. Barne snuck out early to avoid saying goodbye to anyone. He thought this would give him a good reason to come back someday.

Starting his journey to the castle, he watched all the warriors descend into the underground stronghold. Everything was going to plan.

After hours of walking, and once he knew he was alone, he decided to take a short break. He figured that while he was bored, he might just put the mask on for a couple of minutes. It fit on his face perfectly, like always.

He saw Neff take a seat at a beautifully decorated table. The food looked delicious, and Barne's stomach rumbled at the sight of it. He wished that he could rush over there in time to share it with him.

One of his servants approached Neff with some wine.

"You know I don't drink the stuff," Neff politely said.

The servant hesitated and tried to pour the glass back into the bottle.

"Why don't you share my lunch with me. I have plenty," he said to her.

She didn't know how to respond.

Neff pushed his food over to the servant, his hand encouraging her to take a seat.

She stood there dumbfounded.

"Sit," he snapped.

She awkwardly complied.

The servant slowly put some meat in her mouth as if it were poison.

"Good, huh?"

The servant nodded slowly.

Barne thought about Hoger and how he would never treat another as an equal, let alone share his meal with him.

Keeping to his word, Neff and the servant ate together. Eventually, she started to relax and was even caught laughing.

Barne felt a pang of jealousy and put the mask away.

While watching Neff, Barne learned over time why his mother had fallen in love with him. He was kind and genuine, like she was.

As he continued his trek, he daydreamed about his parents' life together. He imagined if it weren't for the stubborn ways of their people keeping them apart, they might have lived a happy life.

He couldn't let the folk's army defeat the humans any more than he could let the humans enslave the folk. He was convinced that he was the messenger of peace. They would listen to him; they had to.

Barne planned on finding his mother's pit before entering the castle. Unfortunately, his transport was already awaiting him at the river's edge.

*How did he know I was here?*

Barne knew he couldn't exactly ask to make a detour, as he climbed aboard the cart. He rode in silence all the way to the castle gates. It looked magnificent without the fire and smoke obstructing the castle's fine masonry.

While making his way to the foyer, he noticed that the castle was almost completely empty. The only person in sight was Neff, waiting there to greet him. Barne smiled, genuinely glad to see his father.

"There you are. Nothing like leaving things to the last possible moment," Neff said as he approached.

Barne felt warm seeing his human counterpart again. He wanted to hug his father, but he knew that his emotions were coming from what he had witnessed within the mask's eyes.

"Did they accept our terms?"

"They did." Barne thought about his answer and suddenly changed it. "...not leave."

"Well, if it's war they want...I have no choice," Neff said, leading him into the western wing.

"No, I've come here to stop the cycle."

"How are you going to do that, kill me? Is that why you've come back here?"

"Never! I wouldn't do that; we're blood."

"Right. Well, it's already done," Neff said, pointing to the smoke billowing in the direction of their camp.

"No, you can't burn down the forest! It will kill everyone!"

"Not us. Stone is quite fire-safe. You came way too late. I can't be expected to wait forever."

Barne didn't want any more deaths on his hands—human or feathered-folk. He had to think of something to make things right again.

"What if I tell you where they are? Will you bring them back to the castle, to save them?"

"I give you my word," Neff was quick to answer.

Once they entered the war room, Neff led him to the map table and stared at him eagerly.

Barne wondered if he was really going to do this. He thought about all the time he had spent watching Neff when he didn't have to be kind. His word *was* worth something, he decided.

Neff's eager eyes glanced down, encouraging Barne to show him where they resided.

"They're here." Barne moved a wooden feather piece, positioning it where the camp was.

"Are you sure?"

"Yes." Barne felt horrible for betraying his people, but the humans were also his people, and he trusted that they would do the right thing.

Neff clapped his hands twice, and the robed magician hobbled in from the next room.

"You've done a great thing here today," Neff said to Barne.

"What is he doing here?" Barne eyed the cloud man warily.

"Don't worry, I'm not going to kill anyone." Just as before, Neff activated the gem. Only this time, he positioned it above the area Barne had indicated.

The robed man mustered up an influx of energy and once again created his cloud, which he sent into the gem.

From this perspective, the forest didn't look like it was on fire.

Within minutes, a seemingly endless flow of human warriors and knights descended upon the location, weapons drawn.

"How did they get there so fast?"

"This is how you handle the unreasonable," Neff said.

"I thought you weren't going to kill anyone?" Barne said.

"I'm not going to kill anyone...I'm going to kill *everyone*." A dark smile moved across his face.

The war had begun. That is when he saw Neff's true deception. Humans started cutting down unarmed folk; it was a massacre. Even the ancient wizard used his reaping cloud, disintegrating folk into nothingness. The humans, too, were suffering casualties, though not nearly as many.

Neff clenched his fist with excitement every time a folk was cut down.

Barne fell to his knees, brokenhearted by what he was witnessing. The true power of the human blood that flowed through him. It was greed. They were going to take everything from the folk—and the forest—until nothing was left; it was in their nature.

"You...lied...to me." Barne stumbled, trying to pull himself up off the floor, using the table as his crutch.

"Life is a lie, told by a god."

Barne saw the wickedness Neff had so carefully hidden from him. Gripping the pointy castle marker on the map, he threw it at the cloud maker, hitting him directly in the eye.

The old man lost control of his spell, causing the reaping cloud to crash into a knight—a bloody mist poured out of its joints, leaving it hollow.

Smaller clouds shot out of his fingertips as he writhed in pain. One almost collided with Neff, causing him to lose his grip on the true Pit of the Forest.

Like a coward, Neff ran out of the room, not even considering helping the spell caster.

Dodging the clouds, the half-breed risked his life in order to swipe the artifact. Touching the gem's hard edges, he felt the forest's emotion—it was crying.

Barne chased his deceptive father into the dining area.

He saw the servant he had watched Neff eat lunch with earlier that day. Only now she was slumped over the table, a pool of blood drying on the floor beneath her chair.

Was nothing real?

He had succumbed to his own naivety and missed the deception. Barne felt sick as he considered the concept. So much pain, all because of him. He wished that Bae had never removed those quills. He felt like a curse, wanting to kill—starting with Neff and ending with himself.

Suddenly, he realized why the castle was virtually empty. Neff really had sent everything he had to complete the mass genocide of the feathered-folk. His gall was frightening.

Barne continued after his father, hoping to put an end to it all.

He reached a crossroad. The stairs both ascended and descended, and there was a doorway leading into the courtyard. Not wanting to make a false move, Barne reluctantly put on the magical mask.

Inside its eyes, he saw Neff arming himself with an ornately crafted epee. Barne felt his father's exhilaration upon touching its hilt. Neff tested its swiftness as he sliced through the air.

Barne caught a quick glimpse of the outside treetops. He now knew where in the castle he was—the armory.

Taking off the mask, Barne wanted to catch him by surprise as he wound around the circular staircase. Right when he thought there was no end to the steps, he reached a door.

With a swift kick, Barne knocked open the door, hitting Neff, who was hiding in wait.

"How could you?" Barne said, picking up a wide sword to defeat his father.

"You didn't actually think I was going to play the part of your daddy, did you?"

Never having used a sword, Barne swung with all his anger. His more experienced father parried each attack with ease, as if taunting his son's efforts. "Then why did you do all this?"

"I'm capable of far worse. Would you like to see?"

Dancing around each other, Barne knew he was outmatched with each swing of his sword.

"Why would you want to destroy them?"

"Why does a hunter hunt when he's not hungry? Why does a bee sting when it knows it's going to die afterward? Because they love it."

"What about Valara. Don't you care about her and what you both created?"

His eyes started to change, looking almost innocent. "She was special—my only equal," he lowered his weapon slightly, giving Barne an opening.

Barne had sworn he would never kill anyone, but right now he was going to make an exception. He thrust his weapon directly into his father's evil heart.

"No, I never cared about her...or you." Neff retaliated, stabbing Barne in the same way.

They both fell to their knees, the pain too much.

"This seems all too familiar," Neff laughed.

Barne looked down at Neff's slender blade as the blood poured out of him.

"Feels good, doesn't it?" the human asked.

Barne writhed in agony.

"Now it's time for me to let you in on a little family secret," Neff said, coughing up blood.

He used his hand to pull the blade out of his chest; blood instantly stopped spilling out of him.

"We come from a long line of lords who have died countless times by the slice of a blade. So much so, that our bodies are now immune to death by being punctured or stabbed. Some call it a curse, others feel that it's amends for thousands of years of suffering. Either way, let's see if you really are my son." Neff pulled out his epee and skewered Barne several more times until he had to catch his breath.

Barne slumped completely to the floor.

"I guess not," Neff said, cleaning the blood off his blade. "I did love your mother once. I loved plotting my revenge for her killing my uncle, sister, and countless others. Even though it ends with your death, I feel like I should do more." His back was turned to Barne.

Neff was impressed with himself for perfectly manipulating the half-breed into giving him everything and losing nothing in return. So much so, that he didn't see Barne stand up behind him.

Barne did share the bloodline trait of his father, and he launched upon him, knocking the epee out the open window, disarming his advantage.

"You are my boy after all. Oh, good. I had something else planned for such a..."

Barne choked him, slamming his head against the window ledge.

"So...rry," Neff gasped.

Barne removed his hands from his neck. He felt the hatred inside him. He knew if he took his life, he would be no better than his father. He had to show him the good side—forgiveness—and let healing shape the future.

"I...can change," Neff coughed.

"How?"

"You're right. I can't" Neff picked up a heavy hammer and smashed his son's foot, crushing every bone inside it.

Barne collapsed to the floor, too hurt to make a sound.

"Being privy to the family secret, you also have to understand our weakness."

Barne crawled backwards, away from Neff.

"You want to see what it's like to be human?" Neff asked, picking the magical mask up off the floor and placing it on his own face.

Barne experienced the same sensation as if he were wearing the mask.

"I could see and feel you watching me, the same way you could feel me. Magic is a two-way street. I merely had to say what you wanted to hear," Neff said with a chuckle.

Barne saw himself through his father's eyes. He looked small and terrified. He felt his father's love for revenge as his heart raced out of control.

Through his father's eyes, he watched as if it were himself raising the hammer above his own head. From his father's soul, he felt his elation as Neff smashed the hammer into his head.

*What's going on? Who am I?* Barne thought to himself. He had a momentary lapse in memory before it all came back, as his father took another swing at his skull.

He felt his father's emotions as if they were his own. It felt so real—as if he was killing himself and loving every moment of it. It was emotionally catastrophic.

On the second hit, Barne's skull cracked slightly.

It was then that all his memories faded from his mind. He even forgot that he was in pain. He saw a smile form upon his own face. Thinking it was someone else made him smile even more.

Seeing Barne's happiness upset Neff most of all. Enraged, he decided to no longer hedge his swings and finally finish off his offspring.

"Neff!" he uttered his own name—a tradition he had to ensure his victims remembered who had sent them to the afterlife, if they were ever asked. With all his anger and might, he pulled back the hammer to pound his bastard into oblivion. The weight of the hammer caused the lord to stagger backward. He was more accustomed to a weapon made for skill and finesse.

Neff lost his balance and fell out of the window, getting skewered on a tower below.

# Epilogue

~Kip~

Back in Scutter's Landing, tears fall unin-hibitedly from Kip's eyes, still holding on to the half-breed's black jewel, which he now knows is The Pit of the Forest. He can't bear to witness any more of what Barne had to endure. That is what truly brought the half-breed's smile alive—to simply forget the past, forget the pain.

Ignorance might be good enough for the half-breed, but it isn't good enough for Kip, who believes in setting things right, no matter the cost.

Still with endless tears in his eyes, Kip helps Barne to his feet.

"Come, we're going to restore your people, your body, and your rightful place in the forest. And nothing, I repeat, *nothing* will stand in our way...because that's the only thing that will make me smile...ever again."

The End

# ABOUT THE AUTHOR

After surviving an almost fatal car accident directly in front of a bookstore, P.A. Wikoff decided not to ignore the sign and proceeded to self-publish his work. Mr. Wikoff kick-started his writing career by releasing the epic fantasy novel "Feylin Lore: Reflections." When P.A. is not writing, he spends all of his free time with his beautiful wife and two fabulous kids who inspire him every single day.

Do you like role-playing games? Continue the Tarnished Lands world by playing Breaking The Peace a D&D module written before the events of The Harrowed Half-Breed.

Make sure you check out the next release in the Tarnished Lands world:
**The Progeny Assassin!**

As a new author, it's extremely difficult to get started without the support of a marketing team and publisher. The make break point for self-published authors is honest reviews.

If you could take a couple of minutes to leave a review on Amazon and/or Goodreads, (even a line or two) it would be greatly appreciated.

Thank you so much!
-PA

A Fantasy/Romance Novel

·FEYLIN LORE·
REFLECTIONS
P.A. WIKOFF

A Single-Author Collection

ANTHOLOGY
OF SCROLLS
P.A. WIKOFF

www.ingramcontent.com/pod-product-compliance
Lightning Source LLC
Chambersburg PA
CBHW070300120726
47910CB00007B/2321